Black Baby

By the same author

Holy Pictures
A Nail on the Head
Last Resorts
Concerning Virgins

Black Baby

A NOVEL BY
Clare Boylan

D O U B L E D A Y
New York • London • Toronto • Sydney • Auckland

Published by Doubleday, a division of
Bantam Doubleday Dell Publishing Group, Inc.
666 Fifth Avenue, New York, New York 10103

DOUBLEDAY and the portrayal of an anchor with
a dolphin are trademarks of Doubleday, a division
of Bantam Doubleday Dell Publishing Group, Inc.

Library of Congress Cataloging-in-Publication Data

Boylan, Clare.
Black baby : a novel/by Clare Boylan.—1st ed.
p.   cm.
I. Title.
PR6052.09193B57   1989
823'.914—dc20   89-32187
CIP

ISBN 0-385-26101-2
Copyright © 1988 by Clare Boylan
All Rights Reserved
Printed in the United States of America
First Edition in the United States of America, 1989

For Alan

Be not forgetful to entertain strangers: for thereby some have entertained angels unawares.

—Epistle of Paul to the Hebrews, xiii.1

Black Baby

CHAPTER 1

God puts His finger through the dust of the earth and into
this channel He spits. His spit becomes the river. Because it
is Godspit, life grows there, fish and crocodiles. Miraculous
water! The fish grow feet and crawl out on to the land. Oh,
my God, they are heartily sorry. They see only the dry,
twisted leaves of the plants that grow in the salty damp of
God's footprint. If they eat the berries on the tree, they eat
the seed carrier and the plant will die out. The world will
come to an end. Sadly they eat the berries. In due course the
wastes of their bodies bring nourishment to the dust of the
earth. New plants grow, sweet fruit and yellow grain. More
fishes climb out of the water to admire the beauty of the
earth. New beasts are born and have no words to praise the
wonder of the world. Seeking to praise, they rise above
themselves. Some of them grow wings and become birds.
Some of them grow souls and become men.

This is where we come from. The white mission sister told
us this; some kind of story along this line. She never told us
where she came from.

There is an uneasy moment after the translator has completed her casual adaptation of the story of creation and the
nun explains that she is here to save their souls for Jesus.
Grandma Adiaha, who has left three husbands to nourish the
earth, speaks: "Why? Why we save our souls for this Jesus?"

"Because without God you are savages," the sister says.

This causes shock. The men must fight and kill to be
savage. The boys suffer pain and trial; but women are savage

1

only because they do not save their souls for gentle Jesus, meek and mild.

"How do we keep our souls safe from this Jesus?" Grandma Adiaha calls out. She turns to the women. Oh, they all laugh, they hold themselves. They show their teeth, young and strong or burnt-out stalks of a long summer. The holy women look like birds around a dry lake.

Sister opens her black case. Here she keeps presents, beads and pictures, silver medals and miraculous water from which, perhaps, come fishes with feet. Jesus ju-ju. The women are baffled when she takes out only one thing and then the case is closed.

It is a picture, taken with a picture box, of two women: one is just old enough to marry, eleven or twelve, the other quite old, perhaps three lifetimes of the girl. They are dressed in lacy stuff and sit in a garden full of flowers on a seat which is also made of lace yet seems quite solid. Their faces are very still with only a little life in them, as if life was just a small ingredient in the ladies and not their whole force. Their bodies are solid pillars, their feet high hoofs. They are untouchable. No one would beat them or make them carry wood or water.

"White ladies," says the sister: "when you are saved you will be like them."

Grandma Adiaha, she grabs the picture. "Let me have this. In return you can have my soul for Jesus."

The sister offers the memento to the old woman, but keeps it within her own grasp. "There is a baby," she says.

This is not a question. Only yesterday the baby has fallen fresh and whole from the guts of its mother into the hands of sister-doctor, whom the women call *anwa adiong*—The witch doctor. It is now in the shaggy yellow hut behind them, reunited with its mother at the drinking hole of her breast.

There is silence. Who knows what these people do to the

child. Sister, believing the silence to be a bargaining one, says: "This young girl will be the spirit mother of the new baby. Already she has chosen her name."

Grandma Adiaha looks again at the picture. Well, anyway, the baby is only a girl. "Bring the child," she says.

A tiny thing, shining like chestnut is carried out. Black eyes blink slowly in the glare of the sun. The sister takes her in her arms, holds her experimentally close to her breast, longs to put a finger in her mouth. "How beautiful is the tree of the church when she puts on new leaves," she murmurs, rocking. The baby screws up its face, a sign which the women recognise and they laugh and one runs to fetch a banana leaf and then holds it deftly underneath the child as the infant, with a grunt, makes its first bodily function. The leaf is put on the ground in front of a yellow cur which laps up the newborn excrement. The women then take the child from the nun and hold its backside out to the dog and the dog licks it clean.

The nun offers up her nausea to God. "I shall tell the Father that you are ready for instruction and when the bishop comes he will baptise you."

"In the name of the Fadda. And the Sun. And the Holy Ghost," the women recite obediently and with amusement. They have all been baptised several times. Each time they are saved they are told a different story. "In my Father's house there are many mansions," the first young mission father had told them. In each one perhaps, a different Jesus. In Heaven, no doubt, many wars.

3

CHAPTER 2

The cat huddled beneath a golden fir. All morning Alice had
been trying to ignore him. Cats were liars. She had been
warned of this, but she felt a pang for the beast, having to
invent on such a day. It had snowed and then frozen although
it was not yet November. The ground was daubed with
patches of hard white which squeaked when stepped upon.
Outside, there was a high silence, as when a scream has died.
The birds were brittle in their trees and did not come down
to eat or be eaten.

It was his meekness that upset her. If he had swaggered
she could have flapped a tea towel at him. He was big and
had the marks of bad blood. It was the angle at which he lay
that begged pity, as if his legs would not support him; the
way he looked at her, blinking with sheep's eyes as if to
thank her, although she had done nothing but leave him.

Through the perspiring windows of the recklessly heated
house next door she could see Mrs. Willoughby smiling into
the telephone, a leg extended and dangling a hairy pink
slipper. She was a widow. Before that, so she told Alice, she
had been a bird in a gilded cage. Since the failure of her
husband's heart she had lived life on a piercing note. She
enjoyed the tailored vision of the romantic, could look out
on such a day and see only the pattern of frost on the panes,
a tiara of icicles glittering from the roof gutters. Alice had
the sprawling vision of the solitary. Lacking the small social
distractions that act as islands on the tide of life she quite
often saw the unspeakable. And it saw her.

She was wearing her overcoat. It seemed even colder inside

the house than out. Water rolled down the walls and some sort of vegetable had sprung up in the cracks. The ragged red lino looked like the rim of a volcano under a glowering light bulb, yellowly undressed. Gas and mould and mothballs uneasily coalesced their odours.

Alice looked in the fridge for something for the cat to eat. There was an egg, a tin of soup and some milk at the end of a carton. As she shook the carton to assess its content, she was confronted by a bulging jaw, the shape and colour of a Christmas pudding. It was Tiny, her own cat, who had heard the milky rattle as a summons to breakfast. Her mouth opened to a tragic little triangle, showing bottom teeth, and she uttered something trite. Tiny was a Victorian, petite in mind, vast in body and emotion. Alice had been brought up to believe that family came first, however badly they behaved, so she shut her mind and set the milk down for her pet.

She found herself thinking of poor Mama and Papa. They had been the furniture of the house. Each chair and spoon was labelled for their use. Without them, these utilities became merely the outlines of their will. She looked after her parents' house without resentment, allowing herself a twinge of pity only at Christmas and on birthdays. Today was her birthday. She was sixty-seven. No one would come to see her, not even the children. She only saw them at Christmas and they never failed to disappoint. After her second sherry her cheeks would tremble and she would make her speech:

"I am all alone in the world. I have neither chick nor child." "You have us, Auntie," the children would chorus. "Yes," Alice would concede as a fall of middle-aged lips pecked her hair in reproach.

Later, when she made herself a cup of tea, she looked out of the window and saw the stray, still in the same place in the garden. The animal impelled her with its saintly acceptance of suffering. She had been about to cook an egg for her tea but instead she whipped it up in a dish and brought it outside

5

for the cat. It lapped up the yellow stickiness with ungainly speed and made a wobbly retreat to the trees. Alice was heading back inside with the dish when her eye was caught by some activity within the frame of Mrs. Willoughby's window. Her neighbour was getting ready to go out. She was always going out. She had a little yellow wasp-shaped car whose angry buzz detailed her lively social diary at all hours of day and night. Once Alice had seen her in it with a man, her leg stretched out as when she spoke on the telephone. The paleness of the limb was eerie in the harsh glare of a sodium lamp, full of little lumps and netted with blue veins like a cod's roe.

Alice watched from behind her wall. Mrs. Willoughby ran about the kitchen in a slip and high heels. She paused, pulled up the front of her slip and, in a dainty gesture, shook talc into her panties. She shimmied into a pair of matador trousers and engulfed herself in a fluffy sweater. Lastly, she gathered up some little furry corpse and flung its paws gaily about her shoulders.

Where did she go? What festivities beckoned on such a day? What would she do if Alice knocked and said, "Take me with you"?

Alice believed that the woman had not won her popularity alone; it had been in some way thoughtfully organised by her husband before he departed this life—a key to unlock the world of gaiety as well as release her from the gilded cage. Her life had not always been a party. During his lifetime her clothing had been sober, her expression resigned.

The window went dark. Alice felt a sense of loss. She stayed where she was until she heard a door slam and then the car snorting into life. She went back into the house and waited to see if the afternoon post might bring a card from the children, but nothing came. There was a caller, an old man who said he was an emissary of the Lord. "Hello," Alice said. "Are you ready to receive the word of the Lord?" he wanted to know. "Oh, yes!" He offered her a bar of milk chocolate. "I have expenses," he tipped her. He wanted to know if she was a virgin. "Of course I am," Alice said. "Pity!" He seemed to lose interest then, or heart, and wandered off.

She ate the chocolate later, sitting by the fire. Because it was her birthday she beat the smoking coals with a poker, into flames. She did not turn on the radio in case she might miss the interesting trill of the telephone. "Next year, I must look up the girls," she mused. The girls were historic figures, single women with whom she had once gone to the pictures or to a hotel lounge bar for a "Rossiner". She put on a frill of lipstick and waited tensely until a clock struck the half after eight. "Well," she said lightly to the cat, who extended a leg in the manner of Alice's neighbour, and then fell into a torpor; "it seems they have all forgotten."

CHAPTER 3

"All forgotten," echoed a burly stranger as she laboured along the strange suburban streets with her bag of luggage, her feet painful in new shoes. She was a foreigner, unmistakably so, a handsome woman of about thirty-five, newly deposited on the shores of Dublin by an agreeably social boat.

She was starting off again, shedding the history her mother had bequeathed to her. It was the natural thing to do when her luck ran out, when she found herself cut adrift from root and habit. She sold her radio and a ring, packed her things, bought sailing tickets and a pair of good shoes. She had a fine excuse and a list of useful addresses. She had an optimistic nature. As the world turned, so did the wheel of fortune.

Now, walking along pavements that were bare of people, past houses huge as churches and silent as tombs, she worried. People would be no better here than in the rest of the cold world. She had decided something about the shape of memory. It grew differently in different climates. In these parts people moaned about their dead for many years, although they always claimed they were safe in the arms of Jesus. They employed the gift of forgetting for things that were still relevant to their active lives. They forgot about joy. They cast out the dread so big that it found its own form and crept back into their nightmares.

A thought appeared from nowhere and lodged uncomfortably in her head. What was she about to do but take advantage of a frightened person? "Well, I won't hurt her," she promised herself.

What was she doing anyway, lost in this godforsaken, arse-freezing spot so far from where she liked to think of as home?

In spite of her resolution she found herself remembering. She smiled as she plodded on into the biting jaws of an unknown night. She was picturing a small girl, three or four, taken by nuns to visit a leper colony. The child met a man whose nose had been eaten away and who had stumps for hands. He had a blanket around his shoulders. It was full of holes which were patched with khaki. One patch was bright with flowers and had been taken from a girl's summer dress. The smell of the lepers was sweet and sickening but the air was fragrant with the perfume of frangipani and of African lilies which wafted up on the breeze from the lepers' garden below.

* * *

At the same time and in the same direction a large car made slithering progress on the numbed highway. Inside it, four adults endured one another's touch with a lack of custom and grace. They were forced to crouch together because of the content of the car, a gift, long and solid and bulky. They bought it because it was a bargain and free of worm and because they had been touched by something—nothing as soft as fondness, but the mould that remains after the forms of affection have crumbled away; anyway, some kind of human concern.

"Do you think she'll like it?" Ted wondered.

Nobody bothered to answer. No one had thought of this. It was useful.

"At least," said Marjorie, "she cannot say we have forgotten."

9

CHAPTER 4

The children had brought Alice a coffin for her birthday.

She cowered for a moment when the door was beaten and then fingers fluttered in the letter-box. It was late. She remembered stories of teenagers who marauded houses for drugs and loose change and Coca-Cola, but then she grew curious so she went to the porch and withdrew the chain and opened the door.

It was only her nephews, Ted and Donald. Loitering in the background were their spouses, Marjorie and Andrea. The shock of seeing them standing there, waving a bottle wrapped in paper and a box that might contain a hat or a cake, was greater even than that against which she had steeled herself. Her birthday had never merited more than a card for the mantelpiece or a telephone call. She only saw them at Christmas.

"It's us, Auntie. Greetings! We've brought you a surprise."

"You're very good." Her mind raced over the option of bringing them into the cold and damp parlour and lighting a bar of the fire or crowding them into her little kitchen, which was both wetter and warmer and which only had two chairs. They settled it in their usual bullying fashion. "You go into the kitchen, Aunt, and we'll call you when we're ready."

Muttering foolishly, she backed away.

"Glasses, old girl!" Teddy popped his head into the kitchen.

"I left them behind a cushion on the sofa," she said guiltily for she was supposed to wear them all the time.

"*Alice*, I'm shocked! Have you become a secret drinker?"

10

She blinked at him in confusion until she understood he was talking about drinking glasses. She coughed up a little laugh, reminding herself to smile. "In the cabinet, Teddy dear."

"Ted!" shrilled the voice of an angry woman from the parlour. "We're ready!"

"Yes, darling." Ted made a face at his aunt to convey the horror of being linked in matrimony to such a voice. "Glasses!" he remembered and his dull face registered doubt.

Ted was the best of a bad lot. Alice went to the cabinet and fetched the glassware, which had been etched in a lattice pattern like a roast of gammon. She piled them into the boy's hand and patted his arm.

"You see, we wanted you to know we hadn't forgotten." Unused to gentle touch, Ted found himself jolted into a difficult and embarrassing speech. "Here you are all alone in the world—and perhaps not long for it"—he gave a snort of awkwardness—"and we thought, my God, when she's gone there will be nothing we can do to show her how ... how ... "

"Yes, yes," she smiled. "They are waiting." She hated talk of death and felt disturbed by it.

Ted, shifting the balance of the glasses as if he meant to juggle them, urged her to proceed him to the parlour.

When she got to the little-used room she found that the children had made free with the lamps and the electric fire and there was a smell of dust singeing on its elements. The balding boys and puckering girls were grouped about some large entity which had been draped with her chenille tablecloth. They held aloft a cake with one candle and a bottle was also waved about. "For she's a jolly good fellow ...!" Ted barked out in harsh melody.

"Hush!" warned Marjorie, his wife.

They were all flanked defensively around the surprise. Andrea broke away from the group and crouched to lift a hem of the cloth, operating beneath it. All of a sudden Alice heard her father's voice; Father, who had been dead for years! His light tenor was muffled and weighted as if it clawed through the layers of earth which encased his body, to get to her.

For an instant, after shock had sedated her, she was caught up in the loveliness of the song and the gentleness of his voice:

Beloved star, beloved star, thou art so near and yet so far . . .

And then Andrea whisked off the cloth and she found that she was staring at a coffin.

Her arm shot out to clutch at Ted's and one of the glasses that had been balanced there bounced away and splintered noisily on the fireplace.

"It's a gramophone, Auntie," Donald said. "An old-fashioned one so you can play all Grandad's seventy-eights. It was a bargain because of its age but it's very solid."

"She's crying!" Marjorie noted with satisfaction.

"She's moved," Andrea approved, turning from the jaundiced wood of the long box.

"Come and let us show you how it works, Auntie," said practical Donald, taking her by the hand.

She pulled back her hand as if it had been scalded and clutched it to her breast.

Someone pressed a sherry into her grasp and she crammed that against her trembling mouth and gulped it down. It prowled uneasily on her chest and she knew that later on she would be sick.

"Come on, Auntie dear, have a piece of cake!"

Alice was unable to move. She stood transfixed, the sherry glass in her hand, and stared at this cold wooden case which contained her father.

"She's not used to surprises," she heard one of the children say. "She's not used to anyone spending money on her."

"It's only an old gramophone," Ted reassured her. "It didn't cost the earth."

"We'd best leave her. She's had enough excitement for tonight."

Her father had sung himself to sleep but there were a few seconds' uneasy turning up of grit before his box was restored to silence.

One by one the children filed past her. She felt their lips patting her hair and sensed them pausing in the door behind her and then they were gone.

She walked over to the coffin and steeled herself to lift the lid. What if her father was there—what if he really was there? "Nonsense, Alice, it's only an old gramophone," she scolded herself. What if she raised the lid and he was not there?

"I am all alone in the world. I have neither chick nor child." Too late she remembered to recite the speech she always made when the children were there, to assure them of a place in her will. She sat down beside the fitment as one sits at a deathbed, poised but patient, her shoulders hunched against the onslaught of the clocks. A single candle on her birthday cake kept skittish vigil until a prowling draught knocked its head off.

It was not, in fact, the clocks that disturbed her. She had slid into a prickly doze when she was alarmed by a bright banging on the door. "The children!" she thought in relief. "They've come back." This time she would make them properly welcome. She would cut the cake and make her speech.

She opened the door with a smile and was astonished to find that her first fear was now realised. She was grinning at a hooligan. "What ...?" She raised a hand to conceal her trembling mouth.

"Home," the vandal said softly and it peered into her dark hall to assess the valuables.

Normally Alice kept a chain on the door in case of such surprise visits but the children had let themselves out and she had neglected to secure the door. Her heart was thumping like a dog's tail. She could not see properly. She had not put on her spectacles, nor the light. "Go away," she said. "You cannot come in. I am engaged."

For a moment the burglar looked doubtful and Alice experienced a confusing pang. It was, after all, a human being. She would not mind parting with a few notes from her wardrobe if he would stay and have tea with her and defend her against her dead father's outbursts.

"Let me in, now," the hoodlum growled. "My feet hurt."

Alice felt she hadn't a choice in the matter. The intruder already had a foot in the door. He was a substantial fellow. She would be no match for him in wind or limb. She stepped back and whispered a quick and faithless Hail Mary, hoping that the assault with cosh or gun would be swift and painless.

Instead of the blow on the head she had anticipated, she was surprised to find herself walloped on the cheek by a pair of meaty lips. She let out a wail of indignant surprise like a cat trapped underfoot of its owner. For she knew by the softness of the kiss that the lips belonged to a woman.

CHAPTER 5

For a while, Alice had the sensation, not unpleasant, that she was dancing with a bear. When she grappled with the intruder she was absorbed into a firm and almost comforting embrace.

"Let me go!" She made a determined show of aggravation. "I shall call my husband."

The woman released her. Deprived of the burglar's ebullient breast, her head quivered. She sensed, in the darkness, a gleaming grin. "You've got a husband?" The second syllable of "husband" hummed away like a saw. "I never thought of that. Well, I suppose it's not so strange." Alice looked uncomfortable.

"He's sleeping?" said the woman with a kind of coyness. "Hey, husband? Are you asleep?" she called softly to the roof and she displayed her teeth in teasing mirth. They both waited until the stranger said, "There's no one there."

"I have no husband." Alice felt a grievance with the admission, against some unknown fellow, skulking in the byways of fate, who might have come to her aid.

"Mother of grace, don't look like that." The burglar laughed. "Marriage is like drinking gin—a little buzz and a long hangover."

It was this heresy more than any imminent threat to her person that provoked Alice to action. She reached behind her for a sturdy weapon which she knew to be there and with her free hand fumbled for a light switch. "What right have you to speak of marriage? My parents had a wonderful marriage. Back away now or I shall dash out your brains with my father's walking stick."

15

Brightness discovered Alice, not with the good hard ebony cane she had intended to select from the hall-stand, but with a flimsy striped umbrella, the handle whittled to the head of a mallard, and it unmasked the marauder as a woman in early middle age, a handsome woman solidly wreathed in flesh; and black.

"Who are you?" Alice kept a grip on the duck's beak but her face showed a fear which had several sources.

"I am your daughter in Christ."

"You are a madwoman who should be locked up. I have not enjoyed the married state. I have neither chick nor child."

"I will call them my people which were not my people; and her beloved, which was not beloved," the woman said.

"Nonsense! I will not listen." She could not help but look. The woman had the pouting and puzzled face of a child and the body of an amazon. Whether by accident or design she was dressed to exhibit, individually, its features. She had an old anorak which was partly unzipped and, underneath it, a thin blouse of embroidered cotton, drawn at the neckline with red strings. Beneath this, one could see clearly, she was as God had made her (a thought in itself disturbing). A black leather skirt curved like an iron cooking pot over ripe hips and she had red high-heeled shoes. Everything about her was unnerving, but nothing more so than her expression. She was looking at Alice with interest—and trust.

"Ten seconds," Alice's voice quavered. "I will give you ten seconds." She was cold and tired. It was her birthday. A tear came from nowhere and busied itself on her cheek.

"You cry a lot," the visitor commented. "I heard you crying before I came in. I waited outside your window and I listened. You were in there all alone in the dark and you were crying."

"It's my birthday," Alice sniffed. "They gave me a coffin."

· "It's useful."

"In fact, of course, it was a gramophone—a gift from the children, my nephews and their wives. My father was a

16

singer. It's for playing his old recordings."

"Haven't you any modern records?"

"My brother's boys! They bought it to surprise me."

Now that the hall was illuminated the black woman stepped into it and looked all around. She picked up an ornament from a stand, a blackamoor holding a container of dried grasses. Her face was restless and alert as if she detected some threatening sound although more likely she was assessing the swag. "My father," Alice insisted, "was very dear to me. Hearing his voice, it brought me back. His life, his death! Tell me!" She reclaimed the stranger's attention with a new, sharp voice into which she had forced little bits of laughter. "Do you believe that the spirits of the dead live on?"

"Oh, yes."

"Do you? Come and have some cake. Would you care to hear my father singing?"

The black woman set down the ornamental figure carefully. She looked as though she was going to speak but instead she nodded and followed Alice into the drawing room. Alice fussed with glasses. She lit a lamp and turned to inspect the stranger in this new setting. The woman peered all around as an animal does, or someone newly landed on a foreign shore. Alice cut up her birthday cake and held out the plate. She poured a glass of sherry. The visitor munched the cake, standing, and Alice used the protection of her company to approach the gramophone.

They stood over the dusty tenor. The burglar was obediently attentive, her plump lips pursed and dusted with crumbs. She waited until the music ended and then she chose another slice of cake. After a time she began to talk about the spirits. "I knew a man got a bad spirit up his rectum."

"How could you tell?" Alice asked and was immediately sorry.

"A beam of light shone out of his backside."

How could you see, she wondered, but did not ask.

17

"They had to get the spirit doctor. He cast out the devil with a big long spear."

"The spirits are not made of flesh and blood," Alice remarked.

"Oh yes, there was blood."

"What did he do?"

"He pushed the spear right up into that devil."

Dismayingly, Alice got the drift. "You knew the man?"

"Oh yes. I heard about him."

Alice's eye was drawn again to the whirling black wafer into which was compressed her father's accomplishment, his essence, as Christ was reputed to be essential (body and blood, she recalled uneasily) to the eucharistic wafer. "Why did he come back? I prayed for him. I thought he was at rest."

"Maybe he heard you. He might have missed you. Perhaps he came to you for comfort."

"I am talking nonsense. I'm a bit upset."

"Maybe he came to comfort you. Maybe he sent me to comfort you."

Alice gave an insincere little laugh. "And how do you propose to do that?" She arranged herself primly on the sofa.

"I bring you astonishing news," the black woman said. Alice's eyes pleaded and warned: a stiff little woman who had once been a stiff little girl. Watching her the visitor was aware that she also was being assessed. She had not been asked to sit down. Her feet were killing her. "She thinks I am ridiculous," she decided and was knocked off guard by a wave of self-pity. "Well, beggars can't be choosers." Briskly she opened her handbag and removed a tattered copy of the New Testament, in the Authorised version. "I am collecting for the missions," she said. "The Sisters of the Good Shepherd brought the word of Jesus to my own country and to myself and now they have sent me to promote the word and to see if Christian people have any small sum of money to spare for them."

Alice took the book from her and inspected it. Her face tightened and grew grim. "You are a fraud! This is the King James version of the gospel—for Protestants. As Catholic children we were forbidden to read it."

"I am not a fraud!" the woman said and added rashly, "I'll prove it."

"How do you intend to do that?"

The woman looked at her intently for a while and Alice began to believe she really had something astonishing to reveal, but then she smiled and said, "I'll sing you a song."

Alice had a passing notion of African music. She expected something tribal and savage, a formless tune, lines that sounded as if they had been sliced off and folded in on each other. Instead, her visitor joined her hands across her lap and sang in a voice that was thin and high and bewitching:

"Thank you for the world so sweet,
thank you for the food we eat,
thank you for the birds that sing,
thank you, God, for everything."

It was a kind of recitation, something learnt in anticipation of reward. The effect was almost as disturbing as poor father's singing. "Oh, my Lord," the woman squealed and she fanned herself. She waltzed towards Alice, her face full of happy teeth and vanishing eyes. "Musta been the sherry. I forgot myself."

Alice said carefully: "What is it like, Dinah, your country?"

"Why do you call me that?"

"Dinah? It's your name. You said so."

"I never said. What country do you mean?"

"Africa, of course."

Dinah shrugged. "Everything that can rust, rusts. Everything that can grow, grows." She spoke in the sing-song way with which she had intoned the hymn. "Tell me about you?"

She sat on the edge of the sofa next to Alice "How old are you?"

"I'm sixty-seven."

"You look older. What has your life been like?"

"I have no complaints. I lived with my parents. I looked after them when they were getting on."

"They were lucky."

"It is I who count my blessings. My parents were the salt of the earth."

"Salt is bad for the heart."

Alice began to be annoyed. "Look here! I really have no idea who you are or why you have come here."

"You asked me in."

"Be off with you, now." Alice spoke softly, with Mama's outrage.

Dinah's blunt fingers touched her arms. "Tell you what! Let me have ten pounds."

"Please do not touch me. I am alone, as you are aware. If you choose to take the furniture, there is little I can do to deter you. If you have an accomplice outside you might as well whistle that the coast is clear. Try to hurt me and I shall summon help from abroad."

"What are you afraid of? I won't hurt you. I am Dinah. You named me."

"I shall call the police," she said uncertainly. Those bluff young navy-blue men would stay all night drinking tea and then tell her to get herself a dog.

"Don't do that," Dinah said.

Alice felt unnerved, unsure of her ground, although she was clearly in the right. She moved to the telephone and lifted the receiver. Her action was interrupted not by Dinah's plea but by the intrusion of a fresh commotion. "CLOONNNG!" The house shook with a massive resonance that caused Dinah's body to jerk as if raked by gunfire. The first of Father's clocks had commenced the chimes of midnight.

There were thirteen of them, deliberately kept out of time so that the whole fearful din did not go off at once. Ting, ting, ting! A little brass clock with a sting like a mosquito. Brang, brang, bingbong, bingbong, plook, plook, plook. At a certain point the chimes overlapped and held frenzied conference in their assorted languages while an old cuckoo clock hiccoughed miserably.

The chimes died. The black woman looked haunted. "Now you tell me about spirits," she said.

"Father's clocks."

"Voices of the dead," said Dinah.

"Hell's bells," Alice remembered Mother's name for the timepieces.

"Oh, yes." Dinah had risen to her feet. "I must be going now."

"Going? Where?"

"Somewhere."

"It is a cruel night."

"It's cold. It means no harm."

The light in the room was the colour of flypaper, the atmosphere both stifling and chilling. For a moment Dinah succumbed. With a sigh she wilted on to the edge of the sofa. "Why d'you call me Dinah?" she said. "What sort of a name is that?"

"I did not name you. I have never named anything except a doll. I had a doll once. It was called Dinah."

The recollection came unexpectedly but Alice barely felt its impact. Something else had struck her. She had just had a conversation with this odd stranger, had spoken of her feelings and her fears, as she had not done with anyone in years. "You could stay." She looked at her feet. "Just one night."

But Dinah shook her head. Awkwardly Alice fumbled at her bag and produced a ten pound note. The woman said a gruff "thank you" and walked away, swallowing up all the life out of the house. Alice watched her out of the window, hobbling on her high heels, carrying the suitcase which Alice had not earlier noticed. So she had been hoping to stay! Alice made an effort to draw her back—but only in her mind. She called up fragments of their interesting talk. It was her parents who responded. In the silence of the night the smell of their lives climbed out of old tables and cupboards and bookshelves; pipe tobacco, ointments, old age. "Salt of the earth," she murmured quickly.

She wound the clocks. The big ones formed a queue in the hall, which received foggy light through a white glass shade. The chains made a sawing noise, louder than the drone and tattle of the clocks' gizzards.

As a child she had found the clocks enchanting. She bestowed on them names and faces and identified rhymes and mottoes in their rhythms. Now she saw them as a lot of rather noisy furniture. When she was lively and busy they hummed quite merrily. If she was off peak they could turn on her and become spiteful.

"Where will she go?" She paused to worry. "What has it to do with me, the raving of a poor deluded creature?" she amended angrily, working the chains of the clock with speed to be finished.

"Spinster, spinster, spinster," ticked the worm-eaten grand-mother under its breath.

CHAPTER 6

The black woman walked until she reached a house called *Chez Nous*, with a sign for bed and breakfast. "Our house," she translated without conviction. Her mother had been taught French by a missionary nun.

Her knocking brought an angry response, a woman in a nightgown who said, "Do you know what time it is? It is after midnight." She studied her rudely, disapproving of her skin. "No coloureds," she added, with a note of excitement in her voice.

Dinah did not mind this. She did not like the shade of the landlady's complexion, which was the yellow of yams. "I will pay in advance. I will make no noise," she said.

"Ten pounds!" The boarding house owner took the money and put it away before properly opening the door.

She carried her case up to the room, switched on the light and pulled across curtains which skidded on metal rings but did not meet. On the high ceiling was a white lampshade, curved like a maggot. It was a fugitive's place, cold and bare of human history. She sat on the bed and let her shoes fall off.

Alice's house had been full of stories. Each object had its memory. And Alice? She was a box, full of stuff, which had thrown away its own key.

She opened her handbag and emptied the contents on to the bed: her copy of the New Testament, a heavy spanner, some letters and a few pound notes and all the usual para-phernalia of a woman's bag. Why had she not carried through her plan and done what she had set out to do? Why did she ever bring along that blasted book? She, a proper Catholic and all, to have been foxed by a Protestant gospel! It had been given to her as a present by an old Jew who ran a small business in loans and securities close to where she used to live. She was looking for an advance of money, meaning to pay it back sometime when she was in the vicinity, but he saw that her prospects were poor and turned her down. "No hard feelings?" He was anxious not to give offence. "Here! Let me give you a little something for nothing—a present! A customer left it with me. Second best book I ever read."

She believed in God. How could one not give in to such temptation? She believed also in the spirits of the dead and of trees and in the lively power of ju-ju. She had a good Catholic's superstitious awe of nuns.

Sister Mary Bernadette, Sister Philomena, Sister Marie Therese. What were they? Not sisters, for they did not squabble and steal one another's clothes. Brides of Christ, they called themselves, but no man, not even Christ, would look at them in their dark dresses with white shields that hid their breasts. She thought they were like the talking animals of children's stories, awkward and powerful, wise, poetic, prejudiced. She saw them like those antarctic birds, penguins; unlikely as snow in that steamy, primordial world.

Now it was the little girl she saw, darting between their dark wings, smelling the soapy scent that came down from their arms, which she always thought of as sanctifying grace.

What had the child been to them? Not quite a person, for people were white; a soul for Jesus, enrobed in the most accessible of human coverings—a child—that which was denied to their white hands and wimpled bosoms. The consolation of the flesh.

CHAPTER 7

In the night Alice had a dream. She was a little girl again in the playroom, rocking a cradle which would soon hold a baby. There was a circular satin cushion on a chair and she took this and arranged it in the crib. In the dream the cushion became a fried egg which she, her normal old self, was serving to the cat. As the animal extended its muzzle to appraise the morsel the white part of the egg began to twitch and flap and then it flew up to the ceiling where it remained suspended, a small space craft. "Ragwail," she heard the cat say, quite distinctly.

When she got up in the morning it was the other cat, out of doors, which reproached her. Dirty yellow, like the snow in the street, bones poking out like a bag of elbows, it had advanced from its deathbed in the trees to her windowsill where it pinned her with its new look, a sideways beam of baleful trust. "I'd forgotten you," she said uncomfortably.

She forgot a lot of things. It was not easy. At the age of fifty she had come to realise that experience comes too late and memory, good or bad, causes pain. She learned to let things go, to refuse to admit those reminders that came banging on the mind at dead of night. It had required attention, like learning, as a child, to eat with one's mouth shut.

She went to the window hoping for a view of Mrs. Willoughby and there she was, in her kitchen, having yogurt and black coffee for her breakfast. She paused between sips and spoonsful to do exercise to music. Her behind, like some firm but narrow gourd, defined by her gold kimono, popped up each time she touched her toes.

25

Alice tried to copy those movements while she ate her toast but her limbs were like the branches of a tree and would only sway very slightly with her body. Afterwards she went around the house, picking up things, restoring rooms to a state of disuse. When she opened the door to the drawing room she spent a wary five minutes eyeing the coffin. Quickly then, she closed the door. She decided instead to go and tidy the attic. An odd inspiration! It had not been cleared in as long as she could remember. She put on an anorak against the cold, hauled a ladder out of the shed and climbed up into the ceiling.

They had shed the stages of their lives there as a snake sheds skins. Shoes and musical instruments, parcels of photographs and piles of old magazines, reared up in mummified disorder. The bundles of discarded fashions and hobbies in the attic were not what her parents had outgrown but what they had stowed away, temporarily, to pretend to adapt to one another's whims and tastes, and then agreed to forget. She crawled about touching items, taking away their dust on her fingers: a bugle, a bat (sporting), a half-built boat. A furry rodent watched her with dusty glass eyes, its crumbling claws poised for reward. They owned their territory. She would just tidy the magazines. There was a sliding heap of *Reader's Digest* and *Dublin Opinion*, some *Catholic Firesides* and, what suddenly seemed in most urgent need of assortment, ancient issues of *National Geographic*.

She squatted over them rubbing her hands together, then bent down to brush fluff from covers that bore dates of half a century ago. Leafing through one elderly copy she came upon a picture of a married couple: *A grizzle-haired chieftain wears a rubber pith helmet for added prestige. His comely wife, bare from the waist up...*

Blacks. She wanted to know. The fashionable term made her uncomfortable. The old people still said nigger, not quite believing they existed.

"Albums are red, albums are blue, but in Africa, where I come from, all bums are black," an uncle wrote in her autograph book when she was little. Where was Dinah's place? How far had she travelled; through desert sand or yellow mud? She opened another issue and found that she was looking into the face of a child who stared back with eyes then dying, now dead. It was a weary face, without anger or even curiosity.

As she thumbed and discarded the aged periodicals she made the disturbing discovery that blacks were not safely contained in one scorching continent. They seemed to be everywhere; from the burnished brides of New Guinea who smeared themselves with pig grease to perfume their bodies, to the black aborigines of Blue Mud Bay. For a long time she looked at the oddly un-selfconscious groups. They seemed to have no special expression for the camera and no concern for parts of the body on display. The women's breasts, suspended at all angles, told more than their faces did. You could tell, after careful study, which breasts had been sucked on by children. You could almost tell which had been touched; and which were no longer touched. She got an uncomfortable feeling when she realised that she was staring at women's breasts.

Quickly she riffled the pages until she found herself in the calming company of the Bones of Thunderhorse, largest animal of the Badlands Oligocene epoch, which ended twenty million years ago.

* * *

She felt a need for someone to talk to. She didn't really know anyone, but she could ring Teddy. She had not properly thanked the children for their present.

"Teddy?" she said eagerly, when she had dialled the number. But it was Marjorie who had taken, and would not yield, the call.

"Are you all right, Aunt Alice?" Marjorie said.

Alice felt her spirits sag. Marjorie was a depressing woman. "Yes, fine. I want to thank you for my present."

"Are you sure you're all right? We didn't think so after we left. It's that big house. You're getting on. It's too much for you, Aunt."

Alice sighed. She wanted to say: I am not your aunt. You are the penalty I have to pay for having had Teddy to play with when he was little and made me laugh by putting things on his head. She wanted to say: I am no more old than you are young. I am sixty-seven and you are fifty.

She wanted to say: what are you up to, Marjorie?

"It's kind of you to be concerned," she said. "It's quite a little house, really. I'm used to it."

"Suppose something happened when you were on your own. We'd feel responsible."

Alice, too aggravated to be wary, rushed in. "Something has happened, if you must know. After you left last night I had a visitor—a burglar."

"Aunt!"

She did not elaborate on the caller's claim, nor her sex, for she wanted the maximum tribute for her courage. All she said was that the burglar was black.

"*Aunt!*"

"Black and blue when I had dealt a blow with father's walking cane," she exaggerated, flushed with success at Marjorie's reaction.

There followed a silence that enveloped them both. Alice now felt she had told the story all wrong. The real significance of the visit lay in Dinah's astonishing news, whatever it was, and the fact that she had called her mother of grace.

"What did he take?" Marjorie's voice was cold.

"Nothing!" She never asked Alice if she was hurt or frightened, if she needed a doctor. "I got a little fright, that's all."

"Of course you did." Marjorie seemed quite pleased. "We'll pop over and see you very soon. We can talk about the house then."

"Thank you, dear, and thank you for my present."

She put down the cold black bone which was still full of the strength of her relative's will. When she turned from the telephone she was shocked by her reflection in the overmantel, seen through a thunderous downpour of the mirror's elderly imperfections. It showed a blurred and quaking image, the wistful shades of feminine longing still trapped within the off-colour jowl and wispy crown of a silly old duffer. She lacked the poise or conviction that make advancing age formidable. Her expression was without the weary repletion of the experienced. The shapeless, blundering form with its damning innocence was that, she thought, of an old, unlovable infant.

"Mama! Papa!" she whispered.

"You're no beauty, my girl!" She heard Mother's voice, clear as a siren. "Just concentrate on keeping your shoulders back and your stockings up and forget about knights in shining armour."

"Ho!" Alice laughed out loud at her reflection. Her mottled self laughed back out of the mirror's gloom and she shivered briefly as a gander high-tailed it across her tomb. She listened for some sound of reassurance but there was only the clocks' snoring and Father sleeping soundlessly in his box. She hurried out into the kitchen to comfort herself with a look at Mrs. Willoughby.

The cat had given itself a new perspective. It leaned against the window staring in, its mangy face and anxious eyes ghostly through a circle of mist made by its breathing. "There's no good looking at me like that," Alice told it. "I have a cat already and she hates other cats. Why don't you try some other house?" The animal did not seem to have the strength even to leave its perch. It shifted itself painfully, like a very old man, and put its face down on its paws.

As luck would have it, Mrs. Willoughby was in her garden, pegging scraps of underwear to the line. After brief restraint, Alice went outside, bringing a pot of tea leaves as an excuse. She banged the vessel noisily on the wall until it attracted her neighbour's attention. Mrs. Willoughby waved gaily and took a peg from her mouth to pinion a wisp of lace. "Why, hello!" Alice said. "I was wondering if ... " she racked her brains for something interesting to say. "I was wondering if you'd lost a cat!" She pointed in triumph to her windowsill. Oddly, the cat had vanished.

Mrs. Willoughby considered the empty sill. "I have had my losses," she commented. "Cats are not of their number. I neither own nor care for cats."

I do not care for cats either, Alice thought. I merely care for them, which is different. Oh, she admired the woman. She clutched at the wall, wanting intimacy, wanting to ask her about her losses. She could see over the top of the concrete, Mrs. Willoughby's garden which was pretty and cared-for. A gardener came once a month to keep weeds at bay and borders in flower and afterwards he always stayed to tea. Alice would have liked to offer Mrs. Willoughby tea but she was ashamed of her dowdy self and her neglected garden, full of things rotted or run riot. Once it had been Father's pride and joy. Since his death she barely set foot in it, except in the paved area outside the door where she hung her clothes to dry and, on summer evenings, carried out a kitchen chair. The garden and I, we have run to seed, she thought. No wonder the children consider me incapable.

She had an idea. She might go to work on her garden. Tomorrow she would make a start. The clay would be full of lumps of ice and most of the smaller shrubs were shrivelled under snow but her father had always impressed on her that the earth was generous. An hour's digging would make a good bed for a scattering of bulbs and bring worms to the surface to entice the birds. Even in winter, work was rewarded. The turned soil exposed the roots of weeds to frost and saved one of the more tedious tasks of weeding in spring.

She began to feel cheerful again with the memory of her father. Perhaps it was his presence in the box that brought him closer. Maybe it was the enlivening company of Mrs. Willoughby across the wall. She had finished pinning up her wash and stood back now to approve a chorus line of silky stockings and ruched suspenders, orchestrated by the wind.

"I have often admired you," she said boldly to the widow. "You always look so well."

"I am sixty-three. I do exercises every day."

"Yes, I've seen you. I've watched you from my kitchen window."

"I even exercise the parts that can't be seen," Mrs. Willoughby boasted.

Alice was confused. All the same she felt she must match this offering. "My daughter came to see me yesterday." It was so easily said.

"A *daughter*! Well, well!"

Alice knew from the woman's response that she had never heard anything so interesting in her life. She also knew that Dinah, friend or foe, was lost to her. She could say what she liked about her. "She is a grown woman now, of course."

"I did not know you had a daughter."

"Nor did I." Once she had begun to confide she could not stop.

"There can be no margin for doubt," Mrs. Willoughby said.

"She says she is my daughter. My memory is poor."

"Does she favour you in appearance?" Mrs. Willoughby's pink fingernails picked at an icicle on the wall.

"She is black."

The icicle snapped away like a wishbone. "I did not even know you were married."

"I have not enjoyed the married state."

"It's not a question of enjoy." Mrs. Willoughby looked doubtful now. She cracked a whole row of icicles on the wall. Alice felt she ought, in fairness, to tell the whole story and was about to do so when disturbed by the screams from her kitchen. She waved the teapot in salute and fled indoors.

It was the cats. They formed a furry ball, black and white, which hurtled about the room making noises like a road accident. Alice fetched a broom and poked at the mass. Tiny rocketed from the unit and landed on a cupboard, where she trembled so violently that the cups within shivered musically. The white cat poked out a wasted leg and began licking it. Alice felt let down by this. The animal had been play-acting. She shunted it out of the door with her broom. It turned to give her a bleak look. She felt she could read his thoughts. Why did you give me hope?, he seemed to say, and he staggered out into the horrible cold.

Mrs. Willoughby had returned indoors. The day drew back into its troubled silence. Alice tried to make herself comfortable by the fire but was stalked by unease and couldn't settle. Sombre faces, which fell into gleams where hers fell into shadows, watched her patiently. Cameroons, Kampala, Tangiers, Grenada. She kept thinking she remembered something.

Row after row of mirthless eyes, squinting at the white man's camera against their black man's sun; mending nets, stripping maize, feeding babies, donning rubber pith helmets for added prestige. They were different, yes. They did not laugh unless they were happy.

Dinah had laughed but when she drank sherry and told interesting tales of anal spirits which beamed light out of men's nethers, she had been happy.

"Old fool," Alice blamed herself miserably. For all her parents' careful schooling, she had not grown up sensible. What would mama have done with Dinah? She would have given her a shilling—no more—and told her to go away and tell her beads and stop blathering trash. "A poor deluded savage," she tried to tell the cat, but Tiny shifted warily from haunch to haunch. Unable to meet Alice's glum gaze she went away to sleep in the bread bin.

In the end she succumbed to restlessness and pulled on her wool hat and went out in search of something interesting for dinner.

The late-opening supermarket had been recently established for the convenience of the flat-dwellers who came to live in layers in the old, surrounding houses. Occasionally it yielded a promising encounter. On this evening Alice struck up a conversation with a young woman. The girl gave her information about the plight of White Russians in return for which she shared her find, a new product—kidney stew with whole pieces. The girl shook her long brown hair, which was crimped like the ears of a borzoi. She was a vegetarian. She consumed neither the flesh of beasts nor their organs. She reproached Alice for having in her basket a roll of yellow lavatory paper. Its dyes would pollute the ocean and damage the fishes.

At this point Alice became embarrassed; nothing to do with the toilet tissue, she was abashed by a realisation that she was wearing carpet slippers. In her hurry to get to the shops she had forgotten about shoes.

"Forgive me," she said to the girl. "I'm in my slippers."

"Don't mention it," the borzoi advised. "I'm in my wellingtons." She showed enormous teeth and pointed at her boots. The comment barely interrupted a verbal tirade against monosodium glutomate, biological detergents and menstrual tampons.

"Why, so you are!" Alice smiled in relief at the girl's feet, bulbous in black rubber. Her pleasure was short-lived. "That orange in your basket, is it from South Africa?' the girl rapped.

Alice did not fancy an interrogation. There were questions she herself might ask. Why was this girl wearing farm boots in the suburbs? Did she spend all her leisure hours tossing personal items into the rivers to gauge their effect on the fishes? The question of the orange led her back to territory she was trying to forget.

The girl, anyway, appeared to be enjoying herself. She was inviting Alice back to her bedsit to sample Bansha tea. She said that yoga was the path to inner union. In her wire basket there were two green apples and a packet of brown rice. She kept her money in a beaded purse worn on a thong about her throat and seemed to have barely enough to pay for her purchases. She guarded the exit sternly while Alice loaded her own goods.

"Come with me," the vegetarian commanded. Alice said no. She considered the offer lacked anything in the nature of a treat. She felt certain that once this person had her in her clutches she would leave no stone unturned to have her gnawing on roots and grains like a caveman.

The girl departed in a loping stride, making swipes at the air with her bag of roughage. Alice felt guilty. Poor thing was probably lonely.

All her life she had been admonished by her mother to be wary of strangers. Strangers were dangerous. They poked their noses into your business and then stabbed you in the back. Alice had been too timid to suggest that everyone was a stranger until you broke the ice. Secretly she believed that strangers were the sugar of the earth, as those more familiar and more worthy were its salt. One of them, poor Mr. Gosling, had tried to marry her.

In her fifties she had gone on holidays to Lido di Jesolo with a woman she met in the lavatory in Arnotts, Esme Winters. Esme Winters was what they called a hard ticket.

They got the giggles queueing for a lavatory which seemed occupied for hours. Eventually Esme said the laughter had weakened her bladder and she had to use the sand bucket that was there in case of fire. For a year or two afterwards they met to visit the cinema and once they went together on holiday. In Jesolo Esme had vanished for a night with a waiter. In the morning there was a row and Esme called Alice a po-face. That was the end of it. Alice felt the loss keenly. She wanted to say she couldn't help her face, she had inherited it, that her heart was where one ought to look, but her stiff face refused to utter such words.

All she ever wanted was someone of her own to care for. She had been granted her wish in the shape of her helpless parents but she too had grown helpless in the enlargement of their ancient wills. Her only brother, Bill, was grown up before she was born and busy fathering Ted and Donald. After that he caught a complicated 'flu and passed away.

Love remained a puzzle. Those she knew whose lives had been resolved in matrimony did not openly rejoice. Views changed, old values were shamelessly defaced. One seemed destined to leave the world knowing less than when one had entered it. Sex—she had read everything on the subject upon which she could lay hands, yet still she did not understand. For all the modern talk of ecstasy and excess, people grew ruder and more depressed by the day.

Her musings were disturbed by the sight of a dog scowling with misery as it picked through inedible refuse from a bin it had overturned. She offered it a Kimberley biscuit but it ran off with an angry look.

When she got home she opened the tin of kidney stew with whole pieces. She liked to discover things that were new in the shops and always believed in their claims. She was disappointed when the contents of the can transferred themselves to the saucepan in a thin, soupy stream, barely impeded by a grain of carrot or a fragment of kidney. With a spoon she rooted for buried treasure in this swamp, comparing it with the picture on the tin, which showed a mound of juicy offal gleaming in a glaze of its own juice, with colourful vegetables winking through. She went off to look for some bread to give it body but found instead the offended bulk of Tiny the cat asleep in the bread bin where she had taken refuge. She prised a piece of bread from beneath her, wiping it with a tea towel before breaking it into the soup.

She wound the clocks and was surprised by a twinge of memory. Once Mother tried to set fire to them. She placed lighted candles inside the chambers of the grandfather and grandmother. It caused a blaze inside the big grandfather. Father smelled the smoke and ran to the hall in his bare feet, clasping his hot water bottle. "Mother, the clocks are on fire!" he called out in alarm. Alice had crept from her bed and opened her door just as the clocks commenced their chorus. Smoke belched out around the glass portal, fanned by the pendulum.

Father bravely tackled the blazing timepiece. He opened the glass front and deluged the flames with the contents of the stone flask. He was swallowed up in an evil storm of black smoke. "It's all right, Mother," he choked. "I've put out the blaze. I've put it out with water."

"Water?" Mother cried out delightedly from her bed. "Water? That it may rot their damned metal guts, you piffling imbecile."

* * *

Afterwards she took the cat on her knee and turned on the television. It invaded the room with its Martian glow and showed what appeared to be fishes swimming in snow.

She had bought the set from a fellow for forty pounds.

For a couple of weeks she had enjoyed it. She marvelled at the generosity of the characters who were willing to lay out their sex lives and sword fights in her kitchen for her enrichment. Quite without warning this privilege was withdrawn. The screen showed only a blur. It was a loss when they failed to appear.

She phoned the man and told him he had sold her a wonky telly.

"Isn't it working, love?" he said.

"Oh, yes. It's working, in a way."

"Well, then. It's not supposed to make your morning cuppa."

It had been like that for five weeks now. "We'll get used to it," she assured the cat. "It's still good company." There were days like this one when she felt quite relieved to be excused from the tension of other people's goings-on. Once it made her laugh out loud. "It's like our lives!" she told Tiny. "Nothing ever happens."

CHAPTER 8

In the morning Dinah went looking for a job. She got a good number too, washing dishes at night in a café, for fifty pounds a week.

She did not view the work as menial. She liked having her hands in warm water and her mind free for thought. In fact she could not understand the ambition of so many to immerse themselves in employment which stretched and wrung the intellect, leaving them squeezed out like a lemon for their leisure hours. Work was for making money. Other time was for living. She was gratified by the hours of the work—ten p.m. until three in the morning—which left the whole day free for thinking and she could eat as much as she liked at no extra cost—sausages and chips and other tasty food.

She went into a church and lit ten candles to give thanks. After that she went to have a drink. She would have liked to buy everyone a drink. She wanted to tell the whole world that she had astonishing news. She had set out with little to hope for but in the space of a day had found a kind woman who let her call her Mother and a good job. She sat on a red banquette to drink her gin and surveyed the occupants of the lounge bar: a refined woman alcoholic and two old men who watched her with hate over pints of stout.

She bought another drink and itemised her benefits—a place to stay, a place to work and a friend. Fifty pounds in wages! It was a lot of money when one could eat for nothing. She had spent only two pounds in the church on candles and another three on her drinks. She could live like this every day and still have money over. It was a good country. Ireland was the favourite country of Jesus and the bones of St. Valentine were kept in a glass box in a church in the city. No one had flung out the welcome mat, it was true, but that was a temporary state of affairs. Once they knew she was a baptised Christian and the protégée of a white lady, there would be smiles all round.

Her own smile fell into a scowl then for she suddenly realised an error in her calculations. She had forgotten the ten pounds a night she needed if she was to stay, quiet as a mouse, in *Chez Nous*. Now her sum for expenses climbed to a hundred pounds. Impossible for anyone to live in such a city! If only she had somewhere to stay. Her smile returned when she remembered that Alice had invited her to stay the night. She would not impose indefinitely: just a night or two, or a week. In any case it was not safe for a helpless woman to live alone in so hostile a capital. With sentimental fondness she recalled Alice's frightened face; she was scared even of her father's singing.

Rising from her seat she made for the telephone. When she found the number, she did not have the proper change. She asked the men who were drinking stout, but they looked her up and down with their little peppercorn eyes as if she had lost her mind.

The barman took her pound and slammed down a pile of silver coins.

"Miss A. Boyle?" she sternly asked, although she recognised Alice's voice at once.

"Yes?"

"I found you in the phone book. You should pretend to be a man. Call yourself Amos or Algernon. It's safer."

"Who is this?" Alice said.

"It's Dinah."

"Oh." There was a befuddled pause. Dinah tried to read some feeling into Alice's tone. She sounded pleased, she thought. It made Dinah's heart melt. Anyway, she remembered her.

"Where are you?" Alice said.

"I don't know. I'm in a public house."

"At eleven in the morning?"

"It's a celebration. I feel lucky today."

"What is it you want, Dinah?"

"Last night you offered me hospitality. I want to come home."

A squealing came down the line, as from the swine into whom Christ had unkindly transferred a legion of devils, but it was only Alice nervously fingering the wire. "I did make an offer, I know," she conceded at last, "but really, I hardly know you."

"That is true but it is of no account," Dinah said. "We come from the same family. I am a civilised Christian, just the same as you. I was baptised as a baby. I ate the bread of life. I don't expect you to remember your baptism but I presume you remember your First Communion."

Alice thought. All that came to mind was an overgrown girl of twelve like a big serious sheep in the delicate white dress with a sash.

"Are you still there?" Dinah sounded worried.

"Yes, I'm here. I'm thinking, but it isn't any good. Tell me where you are. Let me write down your number."

"You can get books to improve your memory," Dinah offered.

"I'm afraid you're barking up the wrong tree. You can't teach an old dog new tricks."

Why were these people so preoccupied with dogs? It's a dog's life, give a dog a bad name; all that barking up the wrong tree. Women, when they failed to please, were reviled as bitches. "Look, I've got a problem," she said. "I'm running short of money."

"Are you after my communion money?" Alice joked weakly.

Dinah hung up.

Alice stayed looking at the telephone for a while. She rattled the button in case it was a fault on the line. "Damn and damn." She put the receiver down. "I've said the wrong thing. I've hurt her feelings."

She would have been surprised at that moment to see Dinah, beaming like a baby, her teeth clenched with happiness, her cheeks bunched into puffs of felicity. She had just been blessed by that most unlikely and delightful of occurrences, a friendly encounter with a stranger.

"And one for the lady!" called out the beautiful man who had entered the bar. He was tall and fat and had a beard like a flaming bush.

Lost in admiration of his turquoise eyes, the virile girth of his chest and belly, she could no longer concentrate on Alice's stubborn mind with its maze of dogs and proprieties.

"I thank you." Dinah accepted the drink. She was also giving thanks to God for this temporary lifting of her burdens. She looked on all pleasures as passing and sometimes wondered if God sent us little balms of happiness as a respite against the enduring pains of life or if the small pleasures were life's realities and the miseries an illusion to test our trust: for the happy times were always seen through to a conclusion while the sadnesses flowed on like the rivers, through many lifetimes.

"Do you care for a song at all?" the man asked her.

"I do," Dinah nodded.

He sang a sad song about a boy called Kevin Barry. He liked it so much that when he had finished he began all over again. By lunchtime she had learnt the tune and some of the words so that they sang it together, bound in a torrent of

41

pleasurable tears. What was particularly pleasing was that by now all the hostile faces of the morning had vacated the bar. And no one else came in at all, all day.

CHAPTER 9

Alice found a little graveyard of tools, blistered with rust, in the shed in the garden. She located a pair of ancient gardening gloves, stiff and mouldy, but surprising her pleasantly with their perfect fit, for father's hands had been small. The wheelbarrow was full of holes and scuttling insects. There was an old newspaper, dated 1969. "First men on the moon!" She read the headline. "Well, well! We all thought we'd be back and forth like yo-yos. The man in the moon had the last laugh." She battened the historic document haphazardly down on holes and spiders and the skeletons of leaves.

She had been a bit dejected when Dinah's voice evaporated from the line, but she was used to loss and she adjusted quickly. Remembering her instruction to herself for the day, she went out to work on the garden.

Half an hour later she was back, trembling and astonished. All she had in her wheelbarrow was a tufted lump of carrion.

She found the white cat in a nest of growth, frozen stiff, his paws folded in dignified submission, and her heart cracked. He had known he was going to die when he went out of the kitchen and she knew it too.

She had failed also with the garden. It would not let her in. Weeds and trees and nests and webs had closed ranks and formed their own society.

Stalks and grasses, tough as beards, pranced like some great, hairy man. But it was not this that sent her scrambling and clawing through the matted growth for the safety of the house; nor even the canopies of cobweb with their giant spiders which ran at her when she tried to loosen the unimportant corpse of the cat. It was the shock of memory.

She saw the cradle. Nesting against the south wall of the garden, half buried under sticky loops of ivy, was the green cradle which had been in her dream. It was faded, rotted, only a seaweed stain of its former green remaining, but Alice saw it as it was when she first put it there, when she had hidden it there, when she was twelve.

The past swooped in on her.

For years, when she was a child, she had hoped for a baby brother or sister. She had jealously spied on mother's pole-like figure, but Mother was getting on and Father had transferred his procreative powers to the back garden. When she was seven, she read in the *National Geographic* of girls in Africa who had babies when they were ten. She prayed it would happen to her but her first decade came and went and the house stayed silent save for Father's singing. Then when she was twelve...

She remembered!

When she was twelve she made her First Communion. It was then that the nuns had approached her about adopting a black baby.

Tiny gave a rattling croak of fear when she saw what Alice had brought in—what she imagined to be the human's prey.

Alice did not notice that she had wheeled the dead cat into the kitchen. What should she do? Hire a private detective? She decided on an advertisement in the personal columns of the newspapers. Shakily, she sat down and composed an economical formula. "Mother remembers. Dinah, please contact Alice." She added her phone number.

She telephoned her advertisement into all three of the morning newspapers, accepting their offer of a three-day insertion for the price of two. She was puzzled to observe, while she waited for their uninterested repetition of her message, that a pool of water had gathered underneath the wheelbarrow, which for some reason she had wheeled into the house. She was surprised, on peering in, to see the cat's corpse, thawing now to a queer thrusting sort of sogginess. "Poor boy," she said absentmindedly.

When she had finished with the telephone she wheeled her wheelbarrow outside under the tin-coloured sky and buried the cat where she found him, under the golden fir, patting down a sorbet of frozen earth, as Father would tuck in his tenderest flowers.

CHAPTER 10

Dinah was in Bewley's Oriental Café, beaming behind her newspaper.

She could not believe her luck at having landed in such a place. It was full of churches and children and charming, romantic men who liked to laugh and drink. The dragon's breath of hostility that had singed her on arrival was a breath of the suburbs. She had accommodation now in a city centre hotel, where a few cracked windows and the presence of winos sagging on the stairs made for a reduced rental and a generally relaxed and friendly atmosphere. It was pleasant in the city, where all were united in hardship and a humorous resignation to their hopelessness in matters of finance and family planning.

Such nice, child-like men! Apart from the priests, they were all married. They loved their wives. Their eyes filled with tears when they mentioned them. "Poor girl, she's had a terrible life with me," her red-haired friend, Figgis, told her sadly, before beating his hairy paws on the counter for drink and bursting into song once more. It was he who had helped her settle into the cheerful hotel near O'Connell Street. He introduced her to his friends, more charming fellows, thirsty and eagerly self-critical, sometimes trailing a kite-tail of little children who scattered potato crisps and had a scholarly familiarity with swearwords. Dinah was completely at ease in this world. It seemed normal to be happy and surrounded by children. The men were impressed by her exotic tint and her acceptance of their offspring.

"You'd get a very good job minding children with some

46

nob family in Foxrock or Howth," one of them had recommended. "You'd rule the roost, so you would." It was for
this reason that she was in Bewley's, equipped with the
morning's papers, to see if she could be accepted, on professional terms, by the fertile nobs of the outer city. "When
you get tired of us you could get child-minding work in
the big cities of America—Philadelphia, Boston," said another
drinking companion. His eyes grew wistful and watery. She
had already noticed that Irishmen spoke of America with the
same pious devotion with which they intoned the name of
the Virgin Mary.

She had gone to bed with her red-headed friend, Figgis.
Nothing happened, but they had a very good time. He
brought home six bottles of stout and they sang so loudly
the plaster crumbled from the ceiling. When they finally got
into her small bed, he confessed that he could not get his
equipment to operate. She felt uncomfortable for a minute,
thinking she was sure to be blamed, but Figgis only laughed:
"Shh. He's sleeping!" Figgis laughed also in his sleep and
when he woke in the morning he was friendly and philo-
sophical about his failure. "Maybe it's as well," he said. "It's
a grave mortal sin for a married man."

"We can just be friends," she said. "I don't mind."

"I always wanted to sleep with a black woman," he
observed. "It's been a dream of mine. We might have a go
some other time for I've an abstinence now to my credit."

She was returned to the task of the present by a sound
like all the world's metal coat-hangers engaged in combat but
it was just something they did in the kitchen of Bewley's with
the cutlery from time to time. She concentrated on her newspaper, folding back the employment section, and found that
domestic help was indeed wanted as far afield as America, in
Maine and New Jersey, although it was Irish Catholic girls
they preferred. A single parent in Dolphin's Barn wanted help
with the ironing and her two-year-old twins. "Not much

money, but you can share what we've got!" the ad read. That sounded pleasant. A barn filled with dolphins came to mind, or perhaps there had been a red-headed man like Figgis, whose name was Dolphin and who lived in a barn. Her eye was drawn to the personal column. *Farmer, aged fifty, own car, wishes to meet lady, thirty-five.* He did not want a nice woman his own age, someone who would be sympathetic to his bachelor habits and declining health. It had to be a lady, still uneasily caught in the whims of fertility. He wanted a child. Children remained everyone's hope. She glanced at the rest of the advertisements. There were several lost dogs, sorely missed by children, an absent passport sought by an Asian and someone called Mother, announcing to the world that she remembered. "Dinah, please contact Alice," she read on. Her heart gave a little bump.

Underneath that was a sinister line which read: "Wash yourself in Christ's blood." But that was someone else's mystery.

Dinah paid for her breakfast, sifting tenpenny pieces from her change, and hurried downstairs to where the phones could be found, convenient to the toilets.

CHAPTER 11

"I remember!" Alice's voice trembled into the telephone when she heard Dinah.

"I saw your advertisement," Dinah said.

"When I was twelve years of age I adopted you." She held her breath but no protest ensued. "I bought you—for two and sixpence!"

There was a lengthy pause at the other end and then the relief of Dinah's chuckle, hoarse and fat like an infant's. "You paid too much!"

"We all bought a black baby. You had to!" Alice plunged ahead. "It was a way the nuns had of collecting for the missions. Every child, when she had made her First Communion and had a little white handbag full of money, had to hand over half a crown in return for which she got her very own picca ... baby ... which she was allowed to name."

"An all-chocolate assortment?"

"Exactly!"

"Did they send these babies parcel post or did they pack them in with a vanload of bananas?"

Alice hooted with glee. "Now you're teasing me. Of course they didn't send them at all."

"Sounds like a bit of a swindle to me."

"Oh, no. It was all above board. It was common practice everywhere."

Now, more than fifty years later, she began to wonder if this was so. The Irish had always had an intense sentimental preoccupation with distant pagans. There was no tradition of nursery stories. Instead, it was the dusky heathen who stirred the infant imagination, sleeping his soulless sleep until awakened by God's love and the magic of His holy wizards. There was romance in these stories and terror too, for the missionary fell prey to foul disease, to the leopard's tooth and the cannibal's pot. Children loved to hear such tales and were schooled early to sacrifice for God's unchosen. "Penny for the black baby," was one of the first phrases learnt. There was as much pleasure in putting a penny in the mission box, with its nodding black head on top, as in spending it on an orange or a dozen Honey Bees. The privilege of buying a black baby was reserved for older children who had partaken of the fleshy feast of First Communion. Decked out as miniature brides and at the peak of financial solvency due to the bounty of relatives who filled their little white handbags, they queued to purchase a savage soul. All the children bought a black baby. Few could resist this early placation of maternity. In any case, as Alice had said, there wasn't a choice.

All the spiritual parent had to do was to fill in a form with the name she had chosen for her child and then sign her own name at the bottom. If she could not think of—or spell—another name, she could name the baby after herself.

Had it been uniquely a local practice? There wasn't anything like it nowadays, of course. In any case she didn't have to worry about explaining it to Dinah. It was why she was here—why she had come home. Dinah was Alice's black baby. She had named her and paid for her.

"What brought you to me anyway, after all these years?" Alice wanted to know. "Some sort of uprising or revolution left you homeless, I suppose."

"Something like that," Dinah said.

"Not that it matters," she added quickly. "I took you on, I am not one to shirk my duties."

"Didn't you wonder what happened to me afterwards, all those years ago?"

"No, I've told you, Dinah dear. It wasn't like buying a

50

dozen eggs. It was more like a kind of sacrifice. They didn't actually send you a baby. You didn't expect them to."

But she did. She had thought of a baby of her own, whom she could bathe and look after. Her parents could not object since it had come from the nuns. It would be no trouble. She would see to all its needs. She would put the baby in the little green wooden cradle, which Father had made for her.

Alice had been the first in her class to buy a baby. "I want a girl."

"God will make the choice, dear." The nun looked beyond her. "Now, who will follow the good example of Alice?"

"I'm calling her Dinah."

"Dinah?" The sister ceased her trading to sneer.

After her black doll with the plaster face, which had been sent by her second cousin, Gertrude. It was the only doll Alice owned. She practised her maternal skills on it and she wanted to use the same endearments, the same name on a doll whose fingers clutched, whose mouth laughed.

"A nice Christian name," the nun suggested. "Call her Mary or Agnes or ... Alice."

"Dinah!" said Alice, feeling and fearing the enmity of the holy woman as she exerted her will.

How long would it take to come from Africa, where all bums were black? Would they send it right away or would they leave it until it had finished feeding at its mother's breast?

How would they know where to send it, she wondered, and was struck with fear. She tore a photograph from her communion album, of herself and her mother seated on the white bench on the lawn, and wrote her name on the back and her address. "To Dinah from your mother," she added. She brought it in to school and gave it to the nun. "So she won't get lost," Alice explained.

"So who won't get lost?" The chaste governess was build-

51

ing up a fury, suspecting some prank which she feared she would not understand.

"Dinah. My black baby."

"You imagine that they will send her to you?"

"Yes," said Alice, thinking it must be a test of her faith.

As soon as she had said it she knew something was wrong. She could hear the laughter of the girls behind her, rising up in little bubbles like milk on the boil.

That was the last she heard of it. At home she got the green cradle ready and lined it with an old wool shawl. When summer came she brought it out of the dusty attic and hid it at the bottom of the garden, beneath a drape of ivy. A month passed and Father put a pot of geraniums in the cradle for ornament. A season slipped away and insects dropped from the ivy and nested warmly in the corners of the wood. Still Alice waited. Nothing happened. Nothing else happened for the rest of her life, really. They never sent her the baby. They left it to rot under the boiling sun amid the heathen savages.

"Do you still have that photograph I sent you?" Alice suddenly said to Dinah.

"What photograph?" the other said with caution.

"Myself and my mother when I had made my First Communion. I asked the nun to send it. She was not a pleasant woman. What was her name, now? My memory...! But of course you have it! The address was written on the back. That's how you knew where to find me."

"Listen!" Dinah disturbed her. "I don't want to rush your memoirs or anything but my call will soon be cut off. Could you please tell me why you wanted me to get in touch?"

"You're to come home, of course," Alice said.

She could feel the blood rushing in her ears as she strained to detect some snort or titter that would let her know she had made a fool of herself. She held her breath until at last she had to jabber, "What do you think?"

"I think my ship has come in," Dinah said.

CHAPTER 12

Following this, Dinah put her things in a case and got on a bus and Alice, after serious heart-searching, put a log on the fire.

Now Dinah was here, sitting by the fire, sharing the warmth of that same stick of wood. Her daughter. Alice felt ill with excitement and unease. She could not stop staring. The dropped eyelids of the other woman were like the polished brown balls on the bannister. She was delighted by the pink of her palms and the peaceful curve of her wide mouth which age had not withered nor time made cynical. She appeared remarkably young—not more than thirty-five although she must be over fifty. She had a talent for relaxation. Since her arrival she had drunk some tea and catnapped by the fire. Her bag was in the hall, still unpacked. These native women ...!

Dinah kept her eyes closed. She felt unable to face that anxious, innocent, limited gaze. How could she hope to meet the needs of one so old, so white, so careful? Her own requirements were simple. She was a bit short of cash. Unfortunately, she had enjoyed a number of drinks in the past few days and had borrowed money from her friend, Figgis, so that when payday came, there would be nothing left to pay for her hotel room. She did not mean to stay for long. The little house was cold and mouldy and still bore the grudges of its former inhabitants. There was a cat like a furred hippopotamus and the hellish cacophony of the clocks. She would stay a few weeks, perhaps until Christmas. Something else was bound to turn up by then.

She heard Alice getting up from the fire and moving squeakily about the room, then the sound of more rheumy tea being piddled into china and finally the supreme provocation of a little dry, forced, prissy cough.

"So!" Alice was bright with nerves. "Tell me about your home and all its trappings."

Home and all its trappings. For some reason the phrase tore into her heart and tears boiled up behind her clenched lids. Lately she had done too much moving. Her heart must be tired. Maybe she should stay on a bit here. She kept her eyes closed and behind them made a picture: a clump of dwarf-sized huts fashioned from bamboo, plastered with mud and thatched with palm matting; home for six or seven people, maybe, and for the lizards and scorpions and flies and soldier ants.

The village was guarded by a semi-circle of palms and from one of their branches swayed an eight-cornered representation of the Sacred Heart, covered in plastic and hemmed about with red thread. No one knew how it had got there. It was faded and blistered, the pulsating heart with its sunburst rays washed out to a feeble pink. No one thought to take it down for the children liked it and the men were afraid of it.

Was it still there, she wondered, clicking against the branches when the Harmattan brewed up a storm of brown dust, splattered with giant tears in the rainy season when the yellow earth became a bowl of mud the colour of excrement?

She felt a dry touch on her hand and was glad that someone—even Alice—was there. She opened her eyes and smiled at the older woman.

"What about your people?" Alice said.

"My people lived near a river which greeted them with its malarial breath, and three miles from a market, where the women sat with their baskets and sold yams and black pears and 'make me well'." Dinah spoke in that strange, flat, reciting way she sometimes had. "Two miles away was the mission house and the church where one could sit and be silent and cool and where there was no company except the black moving statues of nuns at prayer. Oh, and the occasional pig wandered up and down the aisle. On Sunday there was singing, but on weekdays no sound except the death watch beetle eating through the roof beam.

"The boys in the family kept their native names—Isa, Asuguo, Abedisi. Only the girl was christened with a new name and went to mass and that was because of the influence of her grandmother who believed that some very strong spell was contained in the water of life."

"Make me well?" Alice murmured, seizing upon the most homely oddity.

"It's a fried pastry, made from eggs and onions and peppers and kola nuts."

"Make me well," she repeated so softly that it was a plea. Dinah could not afford to listen and so she carried on.

"Only the girl went to school. She was good at lessons. It earned her insults from the boys in her class and from her brothers at home but her mother and her grandmother were proud of her and she did not care what the boys said. She was saving herself for Jesus."

"You had a good home," Alice said.

Home. A squalid, scorched tenement where dead things festered, where the earth took back its quota, and only the disease-carrying insects seemed immortal. Her mother and her brother were both dead by the time she was ten years of age. Only afterwards a doctor came with his translator, who told them to always boil the water—"and the worms fall down like a clap of thunder."

The doctor was sister doctor, also known as Anwa Adiong, the witch doctor. The other sisters taught her to speak English and French and to add figures. She read about the retreat of Napoleon from Moscow and was rewarded, for the waving

55

of a curious hand, with the information that snow was rain, frozen high up in the sky into tiny frozen tufts like lumps of cloud; white as the wafer of the Eucharist, soft as the wool of lambs it fell and formed a carpet which covered all the land, and an animal could sink into its icy comfort and die there, for no one would find him; and all the world wore a white blanket with all sound muffled within it, save the song of the robin, whose breast was red and whose season was winter.

"When the nuns came they grew flowers around their house and around the chapel," Dinah said, "and everyone thought they had been touched by the sun for no one thought of putting flowers outside their huts before—or afterwards either."

"The flowers were a tribute to God," Alice explained. "There was no God in that savage place."

"There were gods in the jungle," Dinah defended. "People left gin and cotton and baskets of eggs for them. Devils too lived in the trees. They were useful for bringing death to unwanted relatives but mostly they were a nuisance and impossible to get rid of, like lice in the hair."

It was Jesus the nuns brought, gentle Jesus with His flowing robe and His glowing plate behind His head. For some reason she always saw Him sailing down the river when the water was like a pale sheet of copper in the evening sun and curtained by flowering vines.

What would He think when He came to the port? Twenty miles along the river stood a tin-roofed bar where sailors went and sometimes men from the village—even her father. It was lit within and rags of smoke and cries of laughter were its current and it smelled vaguely of honey. "What is that place?" she asked her father once and he laughed and said, "Tell no one. It is a house of pleasure."

From then on she ignored the chapel. It was the house of pleasure she thought of as the gates of heaven. She was not allowed to go inside but once or twice she travelled with her father to the port and waited in the cart when he went in there. She listened with all her senses to the noises of the house and breathed so deeply of its smells of smoke and whiskey and flesh and honey, that her head reeled. She had believed that when her mother died she would never know comfort again. Now the scented, tainted breath of the pleasure house began to hum soothingly inside her body, in between her toes, up her arms and legs, deep in her belly and high in her chest. It joined with the music of her yearning and then soared right out of her head and up to the blue skies to join the birds who flew their colours at impossible heights. There it remained, a part of her—her innocence—floating in the clouds like an angel.

She believed the birds to be angels for she recognised their note as the pitch of spirit, except for the squalling, squawking scavenger birds who were the legions of the devil. Angels or animals, she knew now what they were there for. They were there to make us look up, to make us envy and aspire, to extend the cramped imagination to glorious mystery. Somewhere above the great blue sky there was God, who looked down on a different mystery, His world, spinning its bewildered creatures in their many colours; men bound up in many layers of rich cloth, or wrapped in a single rag or none at all; people lonely in palaces or crowded into huts of straw; thirsting beneath the boiling sun or fleeing from Moscow across a white earth which was not earth at all but water turned to cloud.

Alice was still worrying about the gin-slinging jungle spirits. "You people never really believe in God, do you?" She sounded quite cross. "You go along with the whole business of baptism but you still hang on to the old super-stitions."

"Until I left my mother's home I had never met a person who did not believe in God and was astonished that such unwariness could persist," Dinah said. "The jungle rang out with the dread and awe of God. Of course, not all saw the same image. Some believed that God was in the sky, others thought He lived in a tree, or in the sun or moon or thunder. Some saw a penis. We all worship what we admire and fear."

Alice seized the poker and bashed at the crumbling core of log until it burst apocalyptically into flames.

For a moment or two, the house was close to comfort. Dinah could see the tiny crumbs of frozen cloud luminously dancing on the drab air through the kitchen window. Even though she knew they would not form a white carpet but a heap of grey mush she enjoyed watching while her knees were exposed to an almost-warm fire. It seemed so very long since she had indulged herself with talk and thought such as this. No one else would be interested. Alice hung on her every word—and believed it too. She herself was feeling quite contented, looking forward to a warm bath and a comfortable bed. For some reason, she felt at home with Alice. Maybe she would stay after all. The only thing needed to garnish her wellbeing was some small measure of adult refreshment.

She leaned over and patted Alice's leg. "Do you suppose we could have a drink, old Mother?"

At first Alice looked indignant and then merely startled and then a look of mischievous delight lit up her face. "A Rossiner? Why not?" She scuttled off and came back with tumblers and bottle of sherry. Dollops of stickiness were administered and Alice hauled the cat on to her lap. "What happened to our little heroine when she grew up?"

"At twelve she went into the fatting house, where girls are prepared for their marriage. She became a fat, voluptuous girl and her bony, vibrant child self was forgotten so that when she imagined energy and gleaming bone and muscle it was a husband she thought of and that is where her ambition lay."

"So you got married?"

"One year later she was married, to a good-looking, bad-humoured boy chosen by her father. She did not like him because he failed to fulfil his marriage contract, to buy her a pair of white shoes and a red hat. Not that it mattered. In another year she had a baby, a boy."

"You have a son?" Surprise made Alice sound accusing.

Dinah looked at her slowly, as one woken from a dream. "I have no children," she said.

"But ...!"

"The moment he was born, she seized him, before they had time to wash him, in case his expression would change with the washing. 'Damien,' she said.

"She wanted to show him off in front of the nuns whose particular hero had been St. Damien of the Lepers. 'Eyo,' her husband said, for his imagination was limited and his own name was Eyo.

"She took no notice. She scarcely noticed him at all, apart from his tempers, until word got back to her that he had been sleeping with another man's wife and had killed this man in a fight and stolen his umbrella. He was forced to leave the village and of course she had to follow him, carrying the bed packs and pots and calabashes and the baby, for, unlike her father, Eyo had no livestock, but only a yellow dog. Her husband walked in front of her, carrying his umbrella, from which he refused to be parted.

"They went to the mountains. The sun was there before them and its thirst had emptied the streams. They came upon tribes visited by the patience of death, whose skin was dull upon bare bone, whose arms could not be raised to wipe flies from their faces.

"In a month, Damien was dead. She held his body for two days, trying to turn back time for now that he had ceased to suffer her brain was clear and she knew how to save him. She could have cut off a limb and fed him with her blood."

"I'm so sorry," Alice said, but Dinah seemed not to hear.

"The women took him and they buried him. Released from suffering, he looked his normal, cheerful self and they did not know. They were covering him up like rotting, stinking refuse."

Some of the people of the Galla tribes do not bury their dead children but hang them from the branches of trees. She had heard about it when she was a child and she often thought about it, the branches creaking with their heavy, eyeless fruit, flies wreathing the pungent harvest like a hairnet, the air ominous with their dull saw-note: and certain of the Ibos do not fully bury their children but leave the heads above the ground.

Now she understood, for when they buried her little Eyo they put so much clay on him that she knew he would never come back.

Alice found a handkerchief and gave a squelchy, dignified blow. "He was safe in the arms of Jesus."

"That's what they say." Dinah gave an odd smile. "He's got the whole world in His hands."

Alice felt obscurely offended by the other's dry eye. She supposed she was bitter. She looked for something soft to say but everything in her head seemed to have been taken off a panel of tapestry and she feared Dinah's mystifying irony.

She need not have worried for the dark woman seemed busy defending herself. "Life goes on—especially for a young girl of fifteen. She married again—almost twice. Her first husband died in a fight, the second succumbed to malaria. She went back to her village to help the nuns with their teaching and in due course became friendly with a white man, a teacher with a white face and a little pointy beard. He spoke of how all God's creatures were equal, of a plan to share out the wealth of the world. She wondered how such generous thoughts could come from such a narrow mouth.

"He took her far away from home, away from her own country and then he left her, even though she was expecting his child. Anyway he gave her useful advice. If a black man does not change his values he can quickly be rich in the white world. With a month's wages you can buy all you need—an anorak, an umbrella and a bicycle. She found that bicycles were expensive but an anorak and umbrella kept her warm and dry in all weathers. In due course she had a daughter. Even in this enterprise the white man's gift proved grudging for the child was completely black."

"There was a girl?" Alice spoke indignantly, bemused by sherry.

"Yes, there was a girl."

"You had two children."

"I have no children," Dinah said.

Alice expelled breath silently in a martyred manner and the younger woman relented. "Some day I'll tell you the whole story." What would she say then? That she herself was not so much a woman of experience as a guardian of experience, that she carried the weight of several lifetimes and had learnt only that the heart remains a soft-skulled child within the squeezing fist of experience?

She was grateful when Alice did not pursue the matter but asked her if she would like to see her room.

"Not a palace!" she admitted as she led her up to the little space under the eaves which, in deference to its one-time designation, was still called the maid's room. "But better than most of them were used to, poor things." At the door, she stepped aside to let Dinah enjoy the surprise. "We always kept it nicely papered in newspaper."

The cold snuffled around their legs like a blind dog. Despite the chill the atmosphere was suffocating—a seeping aroma of dead nests and damp blankets. A bed in the corner, upon which folded linen had been laid, showed a base freckled with

61

stains. The sepia rags of ancient periodicals clung to icy, greasy walls.

"You want me to sleep in here?" Dinah said, and she giggled.

"Yes," Alice said; "this is your room now. Make yourself at home."

Dinah tore idly at a dangling shred of newsprint and read that Little Nelly Kelly was appearing at the Gaiety Theatre.

"What a place for a black baby," she marvelled. "What a place for a poor little country girl, fourteen or fifteen, first time away from home, up to scrub for good people with two pennies to rub together, and her own four walls to talk to— and even to read!"

"Yes it *is* a nice room," Alice agreed. "A bit ... plain ... but you'll have your own knick-knacks you'll want to put about."

Dinah turned with a look Alice could only describe as insolent. "I want another room," she said.

"There is no other room." Alice's eyes had turned to blank chips of china blue.

"Oh yes, there is."

"There is my parents' room, of course, but you can't expect ...! Dinah, you are being ungrateful."

Dinah took a last look around the little prison. "No," she murmured. "I don't expect. I don't suppose I ever expected." Paper claws waved feebly in a savage draught as she left the room and closed the door.

"Don't go!" Alice cried out in dismay. "You said you were going to stay."

"Oh, you wouldn't want to mind the half of what I say," Dinah said with a sigh.

And, without a by-your-leave, she left.

CHAPTER 13

She went to St. Stephen's Green and sat on a bench by a pond, watching ducks. The fowl, hiding in brittle reeds, made occasional miserable breaks for food that was thrown. There was hardly anyone in the park—an old man, still as stone beneath his defensive aura of dirt and madness, and a couple of students in a chaste frenzy of passion, hugging one another in their ballooning anoraks.

It was Figgis who had introduced her to the park. The ducks' palace, he called it. In the summer, he said, it was full of music and flowers but in winter it was given over to those with webbed feet or broken hearts. He knew a lot.

It was he who presently found her, in a chilled and downcast condition. He strode through the howling grey afternoon as beneath a tropical sun, clad only in capsizing trousers and a sweater whose many apertures and dangling strands seemed busy returning the material to source. She was delighted to see him.

"How did you find me?" she said.

He stood in front of her, his belly foremost, his sympathy sensible. "Through a contiguity of the fates, I believe, for it wasn't you I was looking for at all. I merely came out for a breath of air to work up an appetite for a pint. In any case I walk through the park nearly every day."

"Have you too got a broken heart?"

He studied her with kindness and sat down beside her, uselessly pulling up the knees of his trousers, which then relaxed into fresh corrugations. "Did you not," he said, "notice my webbed feet?"

Dinah shrugged. "I don't think you took off your socks."

"Ah, no," he agreed. "I rarely do. It's an Irish form of contraception."

"My toes are well divided."

"So it's the ticker, then. In smithereens, is it?"

"Something like that."

"Are you in the market for advice?"

"I suppose so."

"Here is my advice," Figgis offered. "Never cry on a dry throat." He pronounced it "troth" as Dublin people do, and recommended a moisturising therapy of hot rum and black-currant.

"It's all right. I wasn't going to cry," Dinah said.

"I have nothing against tears. I believe, myself, it's a good thing for a woman to cry. It relieves the pressure, and it makes a man feel mighty."

"I was thinking about my mother," Dinah said, and tears warmed her numb cheeks.

"Your mother!" His beautiful turquoise eyes welled up. "Come quick. The word itself is fraught with emotion."

He installed her in the bar in nearby Neary's in the special snug which is like a confessional cubicle or a box at some cut-price opera. It is closed off at the back and sides and affords only a view of the gleaming mahogany bar to which it is attached, and the tidal outpourings of stout and small amber expulsions of Paddy.

"I have been cut off from the source of maternal affection," Dinah lamented.

"Here's to the mammy—a wonderful woman, I bet." Figgis raised his steaming glass.

"She is small-minded, snobbish, cold-hearted."

"We all of us disappoint our parents." Figgis leaned close, breathing fruity fumes at her. "That is a fact of life. It is only human if they sometimes reveal to us the dropped jaw. Mother love is also a fact of life. Accept it as a fact and don't be grizzling at its little inconsistencies."

"She did not think me good enough—because of my colour."

"It seems a small thing to you, yes, but look at it from her point of view. With you it's the colour, with me it's the drink. I drove my mother to an early grave, at the age of ninety-one." He paused to make a sign of the cross and his face bunched up and gathered blood with the effort of remaining manly. "I would be dancing hornpipes on the table, with the drink pouring out of my ears, and her heart was scalded."

"Well, I did nothing." Dinah was stubborn.

"Then, maybe it's time you made an effort," Figgis persisted. "Perhaps life has got too much for her, and she's folded into herself. I've seen that happen to people. Remember she carried you around in her womb for nine months. Think of that for loyalty! Is there anyone, now, that you'd carry round with you for nine months?"

"Actually, she did not. She is not my natural mother."

"There you go again! Is it right to go blaming your mother for some small omission over which she had no control? I am adamant on the subject of mothers. They are above reproach no matter what they do. It is given to each man to have as many women as he can handle, but he only gets one mother. Treasure her while you can."

"I seem to have had two mothers," she said softly, "and now I have none." But he had commenced on a rousing rendition of "Mother Machree" and did not hear her.

His song cheered him up and when it was finished he called for more rum and grew demonstrative. "The black paws of you," he enclosed her hand. "Apart from my daughter when she was newly born, that is the most innocent female hand I have ever held."

"You are a poet, Figgis," she smiled. The warm rum thawed her heart.

"I am," he agreed; "a non-unionised poet."

65

"And what do you do for a living?"

"I am an expert on many matters, especially the procedures of social welfare. Now, it's my turn to interrogate. Where do you come from?"

"Where do you think? I am a black African."

"Ah, yes! Any fool can see that. I mean, where did you come from more recently. You didn't just up stumps from the jungle, did you?"

"What makes you say that?"

"As I mentioned, I am an expert on many matters. You know your way around too well. You are too much at ease with our queer figures of speech and our weather and our manners."

She grew broody and Figgis laughed at her, showing large gaps in his teeth that gave him a ruined magnificence like the beautiful crumbling Georgian terraces of the city. "Come on, now! Where have you been hiding yourself?"

"Brixton," she replied.

"Say no more," he said, and she did not.

CHAPTER 14

"Now what on earth was the matter with her?" For a long time Alice stood in the maid's desolate doorway, hoping for a clue. In the end her hands went numb and she had to go back downstairs, beating them together, for blood.

One could not fathom these people.

"But I liked her!"

She went out to the garden with her teapot, looking for Mrs. Willoughby, but next-door's dimmed windows signalled that the widow had better things to do. Her own window told a different story. There was a furred shape on its sill. Alice sighed. Some new outcast had shuffled up to claim the place of the white stray. She approached it and it croaked at her. It was a black kitten with long, clotted fur and extraordinary whiskers that curved downwards like the moustaches of a walrus or an old gentleman. It fixed her with a bright eccentric eye and snuffled and spat.

"Oh, dear," Alice said, and she crept indoors and bolted up her bolts.

"What more could I have done?" she begged herself. She had opened her doors to Dinah, a black stranger. She had offered her charity.

Not that it mattered in the least; except that, on her own, she was a bit lonely.

Hah! That was nothing new. She had even taken her complaint to the doctor, told him that she was sleeping badly and worried about things—cats, burglars, that sort of thing. He prodded her about but could find no specific deterioration. "Perhaps you're lonely," he said kindly. "Lonely?" Her chin had wobbled on the word. She felt a fool. Outside was a waiting room full of people, probably wounded or dying, arteries draining or hardening while she talked about herself. He gave her pills to make her sleep. He said she should get out and about more, live life to the hilt. She ate the pills and, although numbed, still felt herself to be pointless. A life lived to the hilt? *Hilt. n.—the handle of a sword;* that was what the dictionary said. A life lived to the handle of a sword; she did not think she was up to it.

To be useful—that was the thing.

She brooded into the cloudy arrangement of coals in her grate for a while and then suddenly she rose with such a buccaneering agility that the cat, Tiny, gagged on its laundry. There was a pile of periodicals on the floor and she flung these off until she found what she was looking for—yesterday's paper. Folding back the pages she read: "Mother remembers ... " She would make herself useful, go back to when she had first understood Dinah's astonishing news and made moves to reach her. Perhaps there was something tactless in the wording of her advertisement.

"Mother remembers. Dinah, please contact Alice." She muttered the words to herself over and over, like a mantra, willing an implication to emerge. It did not happen, but the monotony soothed her and in due course she forgot Dinah altogether and her eye was drawn to the interesting notice underneath.

"Wash yourself in Christ's Blood ... "

"Well!"

There was no other information, except an address, a time and a date which she realised, with a quiver of excitement, was today's. She got ready quickly, pulling on her coat and hat and then checked her appearance in the mottled overmantel in the drawing room. She hazarded a smear of pink lipstick which seemed to fly off like an exotic bird across the smutted and stormy sky of the glass.

Alice liked meetings. In recent months she had been to a gathering of the Edgar Cayce Legacy and a talk on molecules. Years ago she used to involve herself in more challenging expeditions; pilgrimages to Lourdes where she helped lower the cripples into holy water, or holidays by the seaside for underprivileged children, where she sat on a rock with her book and saw to it that they did not drown each other. She had enjoyed those excursions—the flocks of trembling candles in a twilit French valley; at home, the hardened faces and blackened knees of the infant poor. Deprived children had found her fascinating. They studied her with monkey frowns, asking her for cigarettes or money, and had she kids or was she still a virgin? When she tried to cuddle them they snarled. Once she attempted to entertain the older children by reading them a story by Walter de la Mare and a wizened boy of eight or nine said, "Tell us the ending, miss. We're very tired."

She could no longer hoist the limbless nor restrain violent or boisterous youngsters. She knew that life or the ladies' room at Arnotts would never throw up another Esme Winters. In the gathering years one had to take what one could get. She used to be a frequent visitor to churches and she liked to talk to the saints. In their shadowy stalls she thought they were like traders in a souk, with their brash robes and banks of flowers, their glittering brassware smelling of wax and incense. Now they locked up the churches in the day and had thrown away the candles and matches for fear of vandalism. The new votive lamps were lit by switches and had threads of power quivering within, like electric worms.

She still liked anything to do with God. She loved a mystery. Against all reason and experience, she still believed in surprises.

* * *

The meeting-room proved ordinary enough. Brown lino did not quite meet the cream-painted walls which were themselves ageing to brown. A single dusty light bulb battled against the dark like a good man tempted by sin.

She settled herself into a metal-framed chair and smiled at the rest of the assembly. The only response came from a young girl of remarkable beauty who nodded at her. Alice bobbed her head cordially. The girl went on nodding. She was with an older woman who kept her pinned down with her eyes as if, nodding, she might suddenly fly away. There was an army of youngish single women, rigid of frame as the chairs on which they waited, and a middle-aged woman whose body was gathered about her shopping bag as if it was everything in the world to her.

There was only one man and he looked abashed and out of place, as if he had arrived for some other meeting and slept through and since it.

The door of the meeting-room opened and a vivid young woman burst in, carrying a folder and a little cloth bag. She wore a wool coat in an electric shade of blue. A blaze of orange hair sprang out around her forehead. People straightened themselves in their seats with pleasure.

"We are the children of Magdalen," she said without ado. "Have we sinned?"

"Yes," the audience enthused. Alice wasn't sure she liked it, the implication that she had arrived fresh from transgression.

"Do we repent?"

"We do!" assented the sinful body.

"What must we do to be saved?"

"Wash ourselves in Christ's blood!" cried out the lovely creature with the nodding head.

The redhead passed around her cloth bag and people dug in their pockets and purses for coins.

"We're paying for our sins," Alice thought, quite pleased,

and she scooped a tenpenny piece from her purse.

Afterwards there were prayers and tea and biscuits and an interesting talk about fallen women. "Men are drawn to them as a pin to a magnet, their pockets emptied, their souls drained," the redhead explained. The fallen women sounded like the rough children upon whom Alice had enviously spied in the street when she was young. They played the nursery game of ring-a-ring-o'-roses, dancing in a circle and falling in a laughing heap on the ground. The meeting itself had the quality of a game, the red-headed girl looking for volunteers to go out and find prostitutes. People put up their hands, as if it was bingo. Alice, smiling, found herself waving in the air.

* * *

Out in the street she felt foolish. She had no idea what a prostitute looked like and in any case she felt in no position to advise. People use their bodies as they must. Babies crawl and dancers glide. She executed a lonely prowl of a street of ill-fame, meeting no one except two other volunteers from the meeting. She was about to go and look for a bus to go home when a woman called out from an alley to know if she had the right time. At least she could perform this small service. Was the woman fallen? Alice peered. She merely looked young and yellow and hopelessly cold.

"Look here, would you like a drink?" Alice said.

"Yeah, I'd sell my granny for one," the girl sighed. "Not now, ta—not while I'm on the job."

"You've got a job?" Alice studied her doubtfully. "Good-o. Jobs are scarce."

The girl lit a cigarette and Alice noted by the brief illumination that her job had not brought her much in the way of

71

a wardrobe. On such a night she should have had a woolly but all she wore was a thin dress beneath a black raincoat.

"Don't look at me like that!" the girl snapped. The cigarette clung to her rouged lips. "I'm not rubbish. I come from a good home."

"I don't doubt it. It's just that, frankly, you don't look on tip-top form. You should go home—get yourself a warm drink and go to bed with a hotty."

"I was my daddy's favourite." She frowned down at her feet, which looked like frost-nipped pods in their cheap, pointy-toed boots. "Only then didn't he die and my brother brought in a wife and they didn't want me around the place no more." Her voice was thin and flat, with a wistful edge of country.

"What did you do?"

"Came to Dublin on the bus. Didn't know a soul! I went to a hostel. There was all drunks—never heard such curses in my life. When I woke in the morning my things had been stolen; everything—my transistor radio, my mother's white gloves! I walked around for two days with no clean clothes and nowhere to sleep. Then a man came along and offered me a job."

"My dear," Alice rebuked. "You should have taken it."

"Course I took it." A coarse, surprising laugh came up from her skinny body.

It took a minute for the message to sink in and Alice was shocked. "You're not a prostitute?"

"What do you think I am? A Spanish dancer?"

Given the opportunity she would have been happy to believe so. She remembered her mission to return fallen women to the upright, but she could think of nothing to say. "I'm sorry, dear," she offered lamely. She put a gloved hand out audaciously and touched the other woman's arm. "I'll say a prayer for you."

"Please, St. Anne, send me a man! Bloody buggers don't

even want it in this weather. They put it into cold storage."

"Is that so?" On an impulse she put a hand into her bag and took out a note of money. "It's not much, but you could have that drink when you go, er, off duty," she jested in embarrassment.

The girl examined the money and then put it away. "My mother died when I was nine," she explained.

"You could ... I mean, feel free to look me up," Alice offered helplessly. She rummaged once more in her handbag and located an old envelope on which were written her name and address.

"Ta." The girl pushed the stationery into her pocket.

"What is your name, dear?"

"Verity," intoned the listless doxie.

"Well, goodbye now, Verity. Good luck. Don't forget!" She pointed at the fallen woman's pocket as she moved away.

The encounter left her nervous and excited; and guilty. She was supposed to have mentioned Christ's blood and the saving tide of the precious wounds. Instead she had handed over hard cash and sympathy. She had enjoyed their little talk. Had she been bribing Verity, in the hopes that she would someday come and see her?

When she got home a sense of loss seemed to cling to her house. It had gone cold in all its corners. Somewhere she could hear the cat crying. She moved briskly, putting on the kettle and calling to the creature. She drew a series of bolts and paused to grind an outsized key. When she opened the door an icy gale skirted around it. She was filled with pity for all creatures of the night, for cats and foxes and fallen women—the latter, especially, waiting in vain for customers who had put their loins into winter storage. She heard the cat's juddering wail as it padded in to shelter and with relief she slammed the door against the night. As she did so, Tiny's complaint became a shriek of anguish. She pushed the door shut to hasten to the cat's aid. The beast's cries rose to a

73

pitch of frenzy as the door tightened on its tail.

She divided the contents of the kettle between her hot water bottle and a little glass of whiskey and invited Tiny on to her lap to make amends, but the cat was sulking and went off into a corner where she executed a plump ballet to wreak vengeance on invisible mice.

Now she began to feel a little better. The hot bottle warmed her knees and the whiskey was making her drowsy. She forgot her doubts and began to look back on the evening with enjoyment; the tea, the prayers, her meeting with a real live prostitute and the other's poignant tale of the theft of her mother's white gloves and with them, perhaps, her right to virtue. She was glad, now, that she had given her the cash. At least she had done something—not been paralysed with indecision as in the case of the poor white cat. No, to be fair, she had given it milk! Milk of human kindness. A disconcerting picture presented itself then of the new kitten, raggedly hunched upon her windowsill. She wished the image away, but it would not go. Reluctantly she left her comfortable chair and fetched the milk and a saucer and set the dish outside in a nearly-sheltered spot. Now she had to get warm all over again. She tried to return her thoughts to Verity, seated on the bus to Dublin in her mother's white gloves. Instead, it was the black hands of Dinah she saw, and she longed for her interesting company. How generous the poor were, with the facts of their remarkable lives. How remarkable, how nice, the unexplored company of the world. How little there was to fear, once you stopped being afraid. "We are not alone," she mused drowsily.

It was like a divine verification when she heard a gentle tapping or scratching at the front door.

"Dinah!" She dropped her hot water bottle and hurried to the hall door to undo bolts and chain. The worry had been unnecessary. Dinah had come home.

She thought she ought to reproach the black woman for

74

the anxiety she had given her but when she saw the jovial black shape behind the pane she could only fling back the door and cry in relief: "Well, there you are!"

At first all she felt was bewilderment as she was bounced back into the hall by a series of blows. She hit the wall and slid down against it. Some portion of herself left a fuzzy spray along the wall, like graffiti from an aerosol and for some reason this helped her to concentrate. "Dinah!" she cried, but it was merely a cry for lost comfort for it was not the African who made up the shadow on the porch but two of the most ordinary youths she had ever seen.

"Where's your money, Gran?"

"Tell us quick or we'll bash your head in," the second apologised.

"Burglars!" She was amazed. They looked no more like her notion of intruders than had Dinah. They hadn't a stocking over the eye, nor had they the brilliant plumage of the poor balding young boys and girls against whom one was warned. They were very thin, with grey spotty faces and dirty shoes. Oddly, they wore comical suits, like Charlie Chaplin's, short in the ankle and wrist.

She could not imagine how they had hit her so violently for they seemed to have no weapon and the wrists which protruded were limp bundles of bone.

"The funds, dear, and don't make a sound."

One of the boys crouched over her and grabbed the collar of her coat. For an awful moment she couldn't remember where her money was. All she could think was how the children had nagged her for not keeping it in the bank. They had warned her time and time again about break-ins. She wanted to tell the boys that she would not scream or do anything to frighten them but when she opened her mouth an awful old rattling came out, like the gizzards of the grandfather clock when she wound it. "This is terror!" she thought in surprise. She tried to move her hand to wipe blood from her face but her bones were frozen solid.

It wasn't the intrusion. It wasn't the prospect of theft nor the oily feel of her own blood dripping from her ear into her fur collar. It was the boy. When she saw him close up he did not seem human at all. His eyes were quite dull and his face seemed transparent. "Shut up," he said, although she made no sound. He kicked her so hard it made her retch. "Where's your piggy bank?" It was useless. She could not recall. The boy kept hitting her, across the face, in the chest, with his bony little fist. Mercifully at some point she lost, not quite consciousness, but attention. She thought she smelled smoke. It was absurd, but she imagined a choking ribbon of carbon escaping the gate of the grandfather. In spite of shock and pain the boy's assault was too impersonal to involve her completely. She felt less bitter about it when she realised how little it had to do with her.

The ordeal came to an end when the other boy let out a thin and artificial whoop, like a child playing at Red Indians. Her attacker looked up hopefully.

"I've found it. A frigging fortune!"

The boy put a hand on her throat and squeezed quite hard to indicate the manner of her death should she consider protest and she thought in confusion it was the least frightening thing he had done for it was the first time he looked at her directly.

He left her alone then. He went to join his friend. She could hear the two of them cheering together like tots over her money, quite heedless of the noise they made.

Alice cheered too, in a small way, for her memory had returned and she could see the money, where the lad had located it, on the floor of the wardrobe. In or around a thousand, she didn't know exactly. It had started out as £2,000 when she took it from the bank in a Clery's box. There was no reason to have it counted to the nearest penny. She kept a record, though. Whenever she removed a bundle, she always marked the reduced level with a pencil on the inside rim of the box.

For a long time after the boys had departed she stayed where she was on the floor. The cat crept out of some hiding place and gave a winning performance of friendship in expectation of dinner. Alice pulled the animal into her arms and held it tightly, ignoring the flattened ears and low gurgles of enmity.

She fell asleep in due course. She woke at intervals, chilled and smelling from herself a curious smell that seemed to be the very source and essence of terror. She had no wish to move or call doctors or police or any of the people who control and defend responsible lives, leaving the mad and the violent to concentrate on the foolish. Of course she had to get up eventually to attend to the clocks.

She moaned at the strangeness of her limbs, sticky and strident with pain when she tried to move them. She dragged herself to a mirror and clung to its frame, gasping with fright as each bloodied blotch and ripening bruise became a bite of memory. She looked awful, awful, as if she would never be ordinary again. "No, no!" she argued with her thoughts. "I shall be as right as rain." But before either rest or rain could ease her there was a fresh outburst of banging on the door, even worse than before. She crept back against the wall choking on her breath while the monsters tried to break through. Fear came over her in waves, larger and higher, until one swept right over her head and pulled her to the ground.

In another moment they had broken down the door. They thundered in with truncheons and stopped in surprise before the slumped, squashed-insect figure in the hall. "Are you all right, madam?"

"Something must have frightened her," said a young officer of the gardai. "She's fainted."

CHAPTER 15

When she awoke Alice was in a bed, forcibly held by linen, and Mrs. Willoughby was at her side.

"Where do you think you are?" her neighbour teased.

She could guess from the germicidal air and the rows of similar beds full of people who looked exceptionally well and fraudulent. What in God's name did she look like? She touched a cheek and felt it swollen like a buttock. "I'm in hospital. How did I get here?"

"That was my doing." Mrs. Willoughby squirmed with pleasure at her achievement. "I heard you screaming. I telephoned for the police."

"I made no noise." She was visited again by the dire dismay which locked the limbs and the lungs.

"Oh, you hollered," her visitor contradicted. "And then there wasn't a sound. We thought you were dead. Boys in blue had to break down the door."

"I'm sorry. I didn't know I made a racket. I'm sorry I disturbed you."

"Don't think of it. What is one torn page in the diary?"

Nothing to speak of in her neighbour's well-filled book, Alice supposed. She admired the woman's blue bow-tied blouse, her tweed suit with buttons like earrings, a froth of blond hair expertly piled up to draw the eye away from a tiny ridge of old, white hair which seeped out like a worry.

Mrs. Willoughby talked about her diary and a nurse brought tea. The safety of it! The comfort of being bound up like an infant and having visitors to entertain. She did not wish to think of home, no, never again; the accusatory blackness that greeted the solitary dweller, the empty rooms

78

demanding light and life. She would be happy to stay here forever but for the cat. She had read recently of a man who assisted his wife to her death, out of the misery of a lingering and painful illness, and was preparing to join her when he remembered that there would be no one left to look after the dog. He put off his suicide to carry out the full bleak term of his bereavement in the service of the beast. Alice had never stayed in hospital before although she was a constant visitor when her parents were ill and their complaints led her to think of it as a wretched place. Her own experience was different. In spite of pain, she had not felt so secure and relaxed in a long time. She was not surprised when Mrs. Willoughby leaned forward and confided: "I envy you."

"Yes," she laughed. "I am being spoilt."

"Ever since I moved next door I've envied you. You make me feel inadequate."

"Me?"

"You are so self-sufficient. You accept your lot and get on with your life."

What life? Alice wondered, but did not say.

"Never lonely, quite happy with your own company."

"Ooh." Alice gave a dismissive chortle, enjoying the flattery. She plucked a grape. She meant just to put it in her mouth, to add an extra sweetness. Instead, she found that she was seeing its blueness and bloom.

What a serious piece of work a fruit was. "You're quite wrong," she found herself saying. "I'm not all that keen on my lot. I've always thought I'd like to be like you."

"I suppose you think I have a lovely time," Mrs. Willoughby sighed.

"It seems that way, yes."

"I have no choice. I gained the habit of company after years of marriage. I am unable to call my time my own. I am an audience of one for a man, any man. My life is a constant search for new orators."

"Yes, but there's more to it than that."

"You are speaking of sex."

"I never meant ... "

"That too becomes a habit. Men use it as a kind of flattery, or in the manner of an insult, they do not. It becomes essential to the esteem."

"Goodness!"

She was riveted. She was shocked too, but Mrs. Willoughby was such a lady in her lovely suit that one knew, one knew absolutely, that she was not cheap nor common. "It's so very good of you to come and see me," she said, suddenly overwhelmed by a vivid image of the widow's strange dependence, the shocking picture of some man left with no one to listen to him while she, Alice, gabbled to her heart's content.

"I'm not good," Mrs. Willoughby said. "I wanted to come. I was glad of an excuse."

"If that is true," Alice said carefully, "then perhaps you will allow me to repay you when I'm on my feet again. We could have an evening."

Mrs. Willoughby yelped like a poodle. "Oh my dear! Alice! May I call you Alice? What times we'll have! Let us not delay. I'll come tomorrow. I'll bring a bottle. I've a lad in tow tonight so I'll have tales to tell."

"Congratulations!"

"I am not so sure it is a matter for congratulation. Let me confide in you. I feel rather weary lately. My legs have been hurting. Young men are very forward. I'm not sure I shouldn't rather be in your shoes now—or should I say, slippers?"

They tittered in each other's arms and then the widow looked remorseful. "How awful of me! You and your frightful experience. It's no joke."

"I'm all right." Alice felt quite besotted by the woman. "I'll have a nice nap and look forward to tomorrow. Goodbye, Mrs. Willoughby."

"It's Lonnie. You must call me Lonnie." She thrust out a hand. Alice took it and held on with maudlin tenacity until Mrs. Willoughby reclaimed it. "Here—give me your keys and I will fling a rat at your loathsome feline."

"Bless you. There are tins in the cupboard."

Neat little legs, bravely pinaccled on narrow heels, bore the widow away to her romantic necessities. Alice's heart went with her.

A nurse came, striding like a stork, carrying a little covered metal dish. She looked about the ward, seeking someone for punishment. Curtains were drawn about a patient with a magician's deftness and a brief interchange alarmed all the patients with its one-sided commentary of groans. When the nurse emerged the patient looked yellow and drained as if some vital organ, heart or lungs, had been extracted and was being borne away in the little dish.

With the same randomness Alice found herself nominated for some of the hospital's unexplained routines. An Indian doctor came and discoursed on her broken ribs to a group of boys and girls dangling awkwardly inside their white coats. Her blood was forcibly withdrawn as were her body's waste products. She was given strange meals, a mutton chop snarled up like a driftwood sculpture and short strands of fried spaghetti. Within the space of a day she won herself the name of a model patient. Nurses came and called her pet and ruffled her painful head. She welcomed all comers, no matter what they did. It gave her a chance to talk about her new friend. "Lonnie, my friend—she has your colour eyes, dear— has a suit in a shade of purple that would be perfect for you. You must meet her when she comes to see me tonight."

"Lonnie," she practised, as she waited for her neighbour to return with the contraband bottle and scandalous tales of her night on the tiles.

* * *

The children came. She was glad to see them; of course she was! Grateful to have been patched up before their arrival. It was good of them to bother with her. At first when she saw the brooding contingent of her nephews and their wives, she had had to quell a twinge of disappointment for she had been looking forward to having Mrs. Willoughby to herself. But that was selfish. It soon became evident, anyway, that her neighbour was going to be late.

Marjorie interrogated her to the point of fatigue; her money, her safety, her future in a retirement home. "You mustn't worry about me," Alice said. "I've had my bad luck now. It reduces the odds, you know." She tried to turn it into a joke, but when she saw their critical faces, annoyed by the disturbance of her escapade, some cunning part of her sought to win their sympathy by flooding her eyes with tears; and she was afraid. She had proved herself incapable and she was going to have to pay a price. She wept too from disappointment. Visiting hour was almost over and there was no sign of Mrs. Willoughby.

* * *

Day devoured day. One pain lessened and another grew. Alice ate her sodden fowl and petrified cabbage, drank pink tea, swallowed her sleeping pill, braced her jaw for a smile each morning and lied about how we were; kept her eye, wild with hope, but already armed with a watery foreknowledge of disappointment, on the swing door.

In the corner of the ward a woman gave a sharp growl of anger and expired. For a day the bed remained empty but tightly bound with fresh linen, as if to beguile the soul with a sense of routine. The following morning there was a new patient, fresh-cheeked, tucked in unsuspecting.

CHAPTER 16

"You have a visitor!" the nurse announced, waking Alice from a frightening dream. She dreamed she was at the funeral of Mrs. Willoughby. No one came. There was just herself and one old gentleman. She tried to speak to him but he gestured apologetically that he knew no English. They laid Mrs. Willoughby to rest. Alice watched the dainty feet go down and then the suit of misty indigo tweed. "They haven't put her in a box!" She cried out in a panic. "She'll get her lovely clothes dirty."

Her fingers rose to settle her curls. Had she woken or was the nurse's call simply another trick of the mind, an additional layer to her nightmare? "Who is it?"

"It's a surprise." The busy young woman pulled her into a seated position.

It was Mrs. Willoughby.

She tried very hard not to, but all the same she cried.

"Look!" Mrs. Willoughby consoled. "I've brought my welcome." She parted the grips of a smart shopping bag to show a half-lemon, two glasses and a duet of bottles, tonic and gin.

"I was waiting for you," Alice peevishly said.

"Dear girl! I had an adventure."

It was not an adventure on any epic scale. She had been ill with a bronchial infection. She left a message for her date and went to bed, but he came all the same, looking for her.

"I opened the door with my hair in a net and my teeth in a glass. The lad fell back like a catapulted crow." Mrs. Willoughby laughed, showing gleaming, perfect teeth, cunningly fitted, but when her mirth fell away the sadness stayed behind.

"I am selfish," Alice rebuked herself. "I have been thinking only of my own disappointment. Sit down ... Lonnie. Pull up a chair and pour us a drink."

Mrs. Willoughby made exquisite cocktails. Alice had always imagined this to be a manly skill. She wiped lemon from her fingers on a dainty hankie and crossed her ankles delicately as she hoovered up the contents of the glass. "So when are they letting you out, dear?" she beamed when the glass was empty.

"They said I could go home on the fifteenth."

"Tomorrow is the fifteenth. Oh, I'm pleased. We could have an outing. Do you feel up to it?"

"The odd thing is, I feel up to anything except going home."

"That's settled then. We'll head into town and treat ourselves to lunch. My car is on the blink but we'll take a taxi."

The thought crossed Alice's mind that she ought not further to strain her damaged capital. She imagined from Mrs. Willoughby's clothes that her tastes were expensive. "Where shall we go?"

"One of those French places, I thought. Let's have a beano—a beano with vino." Her face was quite pink but she wrestled with the cap of the gin bottle again.

"Naughty girls, we are!" She sloshed out a second measure—"Just to freshen the lemon!" Alice observed that she neglected to add any tonic, but she could not rouse herself to comment. "Aren't they expensive, those French places?" Her face flushed furiously when she said this for she knew she was being a killjoy.

"Gin, glorious gin!" Mrs. Willoughby crooned into her glass. "Expensive? Oh, yes, darling. You have to go to the top with the frogs. Otherwise you're into drain trouble?"

84

"Drain trouble?" For some reason she thought of Esme Winters and the fire bucket.

"They don't pull out the stops on the latrines. Holes in the floor, that sort of thing."

"But it's sinks that have sops—stops—not lavatories!" Sinks that have stops, stinks that have sops? She was getting into difficulties. Her mouth was like a garment whose elastic has perished. She took another gulp of gin. She was surprised when Mrs. Willoughby erupted with hoarse mirth. "Oh, you're priceless, Alice." What had she said that was so funny? She laughed too, delighted to be a success. Mrs. Willoughby chortled until her eyes popped like dewdrops out of the red web of their surrounding lines. She was aware that people were looking and some sober, sentinel part of her brain was begging her to stop. Each time she caught Mrs. Willoughby's glance they were off. She had never known this with anybody, the happiness of being at one in mirth.

Of course they were stopped. The nurse came and shook Alice's sore arm, quite roughly, and Alice immediately grew meek, casting a pleading glance at her visitor. "I am sorry, nurse, my friend and I were sharing a ... joke."

"That's all right, dear. Just don't drink that stuff if you're pregnant." To her astonishment the nurse was winking at Mrs. Willoughby, who savoured the sister's wit with a splurt of joy that sprayed neat gin upon the counterpane.

"I only wanted to say there is a person to see you."

It was the nurse's turn to be surprised when this flung the elderly ladies into a fresh paroxysm. "Person" was Mrs. Willoughby's term for a man. "Well, I'm buggered," Mrs. Willoughby wept. "Here I come tottering from my sick-bed and you're all fixed up with a person. Perhaps he'd like a drink. There's still a spoonful in the bottle." She rooted around in her plastic bag. "I'm afraid we have run out of lemon."

"I daresay he *is* a lemon!" Alice cried, delighted by her

boldness. The two of them howled like the Baskerville hound.

Dinah was standing at the glass door of the ward, her forehead pleated in perplexity. At first she thought she had been guided to the wrong old lady. She had never seen Alice laughing before. Then, when the nurse announced her, the woman in the bed grew sober for a moment and looked worried and then there was no mistaking her.

In the week since she had read a newspaper report of Alice's misfortune, Dinah had been endeavouring to forget all about her. She had no need of her now. Her financial difficulties had been resolved by a chance occurrence—the sudden illness of a waitress in the café. For a few days she was able to hold down two jobs and was well compensated. All the same, she felt responsible.

She approached the bed and Alice looked up, smiling wildly. For a minute her eye grew vague but then she took her hand and addressed a smart little inebriated woman who sat at her bed. "It's Dinah!" She returned to her with an amused glance. "We thought it was a person."

What on earth was she talking about? Dinah took back her hand. "I'm a person."

"What is all this about?" Mrs. Willoughby said coyly, as if she was the surprised guest of *This Is Your Life*.

"Dinah, dear," Alice said, "would you like a drink?"

"No, wait!" Mrs. Willoughby arrested Alice's hand as it groped for the gin. "Make her state her business."

"It's all right!" Alice grinned unhappily at one and then the other. "I know her. I do."

"I read about your accident," Dinah said. "'Old Woman's Ordeal', the paper called it. It sounds like a disease of the bowel. How are you anyway?"

"I'm going home tomorrow. Come and see me then and we'll talk about everything."

"You're not going home. You're coming out with me," Mrs. Willoughby reminded her. "Who is she?"

She was speaking to Alice, although she glared at Dinah and it was Dinah who answered.

"She says she is my mother."

Alice made an apologetic shrug.

"What happened your own mother?" The widow fell on Alice to share this hilarity.

"She was eaten by missionaries," said Dinah, knowing no one was listening.

Something was not right. Alice could smell danger. She tried to sort it out but her brain kept bending over like a rubber fork and it made her giggle. She looked at Dinah and was confused to see a solemn face. Why hadn't she got a drink in her hand? Why wasn't she happy? Black people were always happy. She was dimly aware that the two women were competing over her. She had never been the object of jealousy before. She could not help but behave badly.

"Dinah, you are sulking," she said loudly. "Sit down and stop making us feel uneasy. Say hello to my good friend, Mrs. Willoughby. Mrs. Willoughby saved my life," she added meaningfully.

Dinah could see the sense of that. She fetched a hard hospital chair for herself to sit on.

"Lonnie!" Alice addressed the drunk old lady whose eye took on the excitement of the hunter when it fixed itself upon Dinah. "Meet Dinah, pal of my cradle days. I paid cash down for her salvation."

Dinah remained standing, her hand gripping the chair as if she intended to bash the two old ladies to death with it. "Why don't you tell her what you put in the newspaper?" she said.

Alice grew embarrassed. "I am your mother!" she tried out in her befuddled head, but even thinking it gave her the dangerous feeling of passing through the asylum gates. It occurred to her that the Virgin Mary must have felt like this when the angel had compelled her to announce that she had conceived of the Holy Ghost. "This is very awkward," she mumbled.

"It's boring!" Mrs. Willoughby cried. She had never dreamed that there could be a drama to which she would not be central. "I am being made to feel extraneous to my own party." She swiped her gloves and shopping bag from the bed and stood up. She glared at both Alice and Dinah before she turned to leave. "I did not know that such people existed," she added mysteriously.

"Wait!" Alice cried. It was all she could do to restrain herself from pitching out of bed and tackling the dainty ankles. To her relief Mrs. Willoughby turned back and rewarded her with a fly-snapping little wink. "Are we still on for tomorrow, girlie? Shall I line up a limo?"

"Oh, do."

Then she was gone and Alice was left alone to face Dinah. She thought it best to respond to that look of exaggerated affront with dignity and reason. "You are too impetuous, Dinah," she said gently. "There is such a thing as good form and you would do well to acquaint yourself with it. It is good form to knock before entering a room and to defer to existing conversation and not butt in. It is good form to respect the prior commitments of a new acquaintance. I had a life, you know, before you came along."

"In a pig's arse," Dinah said, and she stamped off out of the room.

Why was she always doing that? Sobriety swept over Alice with its vengeful gloom. A nurse came to comfort her and brought her tea. "Visitors have no consideration. They have you worn out. Think of something nice and give us a smile."

Soon Alice smiled so fiercely that the nurse uneasily asked her would she like a valium.

"Get me the hairdresser," Alice patted the sparse fluff of her hair, through which her bloody bruises showed.

"Going on the razzle, are you?" The nurse tucked her in.

The cup in Alice's hand began to tremble noisily and tea lurched out on to the saucer. "I am," the little battered woman said intently.

CHAPTER 17

Now Alice was in a taxi on her way to God-knows-where and Mrs. Willoughby's whole fox was nudging her cheek as the widow pushed secrets into her ear.

"I've never told anyone this!"

"Don't breathe a word ... "

Some of the revelations were quite ordinary. Others retained their mystery for it was hard to hear above the engine and Mrs. Willoughby's voice had sunk to an excited snarl. Each time the widow's hand spancelled the bones of Alice's arm and an exhortation to secrecy was issued, her heart jerked in mimicry of the youthful antics of romance.

Like the Little Mermaid she suffered for love. The doctor had said she should rest up for several weeks and she was in pain but she kept quiet about that. Lonnie would have little patience with a misery-guts. She had style, and something more precious, something Alice had always imagined to rest solely within the powerful capacities of the male. She knew her way around.

"Do you know what?" Mrs. Willoughby's blue eyes bubbled.

"No, tell me!" Alice wished that happiness could transform the glum set of her face, but as she sank back into the black Rexine with its hellish floral vapours and stained furry panels she knew she looked, as usual, like an animal on its way to the abattoir.

The widow gurgled with laughter so that her next disclosure could not be properly heard but Alice thought she heard her say that her husband had once made her do something in the wardrobe. "Between ourselves, he was a bit too fond of you-know-what," Mrs. Willoughby breathed.

* * *

Alice peered down at a sandcastle made of spinach around which tiny prawns lay scattered in a pool of red, like the fingers of little children severed in dangerous play. A faintly metallic taste, which was like the tang of blood, enhanced the suggestion of carnage.

She suppressed a sigh.

To be fair, the sandcastle was not entirely responsible for her disappointment. Almost as soon as they were settled at their table in the restaurant, there was a change of mood. Alice was perusing the poetic menu with its immense prices, when Mrs. Willoughby, not bothering to adjure confidence, confessed, "I am not a rich woman."

"No," Alice had agreed quickly. "We won't make a habit of this."

"All very well for you," her neighbour argued. "I'm only a widow."

As a debate it was incomplete but Alice, greedy for her euphoria, said quickly, "Don't you worry. This is my treat. After all ...!"

After all, the idea of a French restaurant had been Mrs. Willoughby's. What if this set a pattern for their relationship? She would be in the poorhouse. Imagine Marjorie's ire! On the way to lunch, Alice had paid the taxi driver. It seemed quite natural to do so when Mrs. Willoughby snapped open her tiny crocodile purse and peered into it as if it presented some mighty mystery, like the engine of a motor car. She was used to going out with men, who probably paid for everything.

Squeamishly, Alice forked a rosy little dripping finger into her mouth.

"Fresh langoustines in a concentration of cherry tomatoes and Armagnac with shallots and cream, surrounding a timbale of summer greens," it said on the menu. It sounded enormous. In reality it was the sort of miniature presentation one might bring to a baby in a high chair, to introduce it to eating.

Mrs. Willoughby ordered a hot lobster mousse and some-things of lamb to follow. Without warning, the compliant little fox was hurtled past her jaw. "Bring us champagne," she ordered the waiter. "It's a selly."

Alice suddenly felt quite frightened. "What's a selly?"

"A celebration, you dumb clot," her friend said and she turned and winked at the waiter to share the joke. "We're celebrating her return to the land of the living."

How much does it cost, she wondered in dread, but in silence lest it refresh the intimate mirth of the widow and the waiter.

Mrs. Willoughby's first course turned out to be a sort of steamed pudding in a rust-coloured sauce, even less appetising than the sandcastle. "It's an experience," Alice lectured herself. "I know nothing about these things." She waited for Mrs. Willougby to slice it with her fork, and for a rapturous response. It was a blow when she just pushed the plate irritably away. "I won't be able for this," she complained. "I don't feel well."

"Oh, try a little bit." Alice could not conceal her disappointment. She herself was feeling quite sore by now, and badly shaken, but she would not let it spoil their outing.

The waiter came with champagne. "She's not feeling well," Alice said, to explain her neighbour's slumped displeasure and her own forlornness.

"This is good for what ails you." The waiter used skilled thumbs to expel the cork. He flushed beautiful long glasses with the sudsy liquid. They both watched Mrs. Willoughby hopefully but she discouraged them with a deathly smile. She did look quite ill. Underneath the rouge there was a wintery tinge and her lips were pale.

"I'm not moving till you've got that down you," the waiter resolved. At last she made a tepid gesture towards her glass and put it feebly to her lips.

"There now, good girl. And again!" He topped up her glass. Her little fingers fluttered to deter him and she gave him a flirtatious glance of reprimand. In spite of her anxiety Alice couldn't help noticing the gratitude of the man for this response. He was only a boy, really. His moustache looked as if it had been pencilled on. Still, she got the feeling that if she had not been there he might have attempted something. She made a cautious movement toward her own champagne, narrowing her lips warily as they met the glass, but in fact the drink was delicious. She was surprised to see Mrs. Willoughby with an empty glass. She could have sworn the boy had refilled it. He did so now and her friend, seeming restored, seized the graceful vessel, which she referred to as a flute, and drained it and waved it in the air. "When we are married . . . " she sang. "How happy we will be!"

"Are you feeling better?" Alice said.

"There is nothing whatever the matter with me, except I am so thirsty, I could drink out of a whore's boot!" She laid her fingers on her breast and Alice imagined the youth followed this gesture with a longing look. "My heart took a little turn, that is all. I get turns. I have been told to take life easy, but life, of its essence, is not easy and I am resolved to give as good as I get. Garçon!". . . She addressed the solicitous boy. "Do I look to you like an easy woman?"

Alice suffered a thrill of alarm seeing the waiter's raw face turn seedy with the effort of a leer. "Thank you for your help, young man," she said coldly. "You may leave us alone now."

"Spoilsport," Mrs. Willoughby mouthed when they were

93

on their own, but Alice was relieved to hear an ensuing snort of mirth.

"You probably think me very stiff."

Mrs. Willoughby thought about it. She pulled the plate of cooling fish toward her and began to eat. Alice waited while the plate was swept with pieces of bread in a manner Mother would have thought deplorable. "You are right," she decided.

"I can't help it."

Mrs. Willoughby sighed. "I'm not complaining. You are my friend. All you have to do is learn to trust me."

"Oh, I do."

"Rubbish. You keep looking as if I'm about to burst into flames. I know how to handle myself. You just come along for the ride and enjoy the laughs."

"I am enjoying myself. I'm having a lovely time."

"Well, I'd hate to see you in a bad mood. I like you, Alice, but you could get on a person's nerves. Look at the way you purse your lips when you drink. Knock it back!"

Obediently Alice drained her glass in a swallow. The ghost of the drink stayed in her throat like a prickly ball and a smile spread over her face.

"That's it. Now, have another."

Oddly enough, the champagne was all gone. Alice wondered where but did not care. She had already had more than enough.

Through a haze she heard Mrs. Willoughby calling for a second bottle and demanding her chops to be presented.

Alice began to feel quite hungry. The pretty colours on her plate blurred attractively. Now she thought she could see the point of this nouvelle nonsense. The food was easy to manage when the jaws were blunted by alcohol. She reached for her plate but the waiter got there first, putting coin-sized morsels of lamb in front of her companion as he snatched away her own little lunch.

"Strictly between ourselves, dear ... " Mrs. Willoughby

diverted her as she was about to try and retrieve her meal. "You could use a perm and a girdle. Break into the piggy bank. Buy a nice pair of high heels and a satinised raincoat."

"I'm not glamorous," Alice admitted. She remembered how pleased she had been when the hairdresser presented her with a mirror in her sickbed the day before. "You must find me dull. I like to talk about the old times—my parents .. ." Alice hesitated. "My daughter." The stark confession gave Alice such a fright that she lowered another ball of bubbles into her throat. At the same time she was relieved. The incident at the hospital with Dinah had set up a niggling discomfort. Sooner or later, she must own up. Besides, she had begun to think that Mrs. Willoughby might not be suited to the role of sole companion. She envisaged a future in which Dinah would look after her when she was ill or tired and Mrs. Willoughby would whisk her off when she was rested.

"You're not dull, Alice, not to me." Lonnie gave a woolly chuckle. "Your daughter ...?"

"That black woman who visited me in the hospital."

"Oh, yes."

"She was telling the truth. I tried to tell you over the garden wall. She is my daughter."

"Well! Where have *you* been?" Mrs. Willoughby gave a triumphant croak.

Alice paused to allow exit to a weak snigger. "I bought her for two and sixpence."

The two ladies began to laugh. They laughed until water curdled their make-up and their cries were reduced to dangerous creaks.

Oh, what luck they hadn't ordered duck or sole! They might now be choking on a bone. What larks, what lovely times they would have! "Lonnie, dear friend," Alice said, her tears of mirth turned maudlin, "I have never been so happy in my life."

Mrs. Willoughby gave a disgusted grunt. Alice looked

down at the pink cloth, ashamed of herself. She had put her foot in it again. She should have known her friend wouldn't go for sentiment. If only she could think of something amusing, to turn it into a joke. There was a sharp rap on the table, which upset a glass and some cutlery. She looked up quickly and was astonished to see that it was not Mrs. Willoughby's hand which had struck the table, but her head. The vigilant glass eyes of the fox stared up from the bread plate, its dead paws flung out in alarm beside the dead head of its owner.

CHAPTER 18

The Meals people came on their wheels with nursery food in silver paper dishes. "The mountain comes to Mahomet," Alice smiled in embarrassment as the two women ferreted about in her kitchen for respectable plates and forks.

"I will eat later," she told the ladies. She did not like to say that she had to share her meal with the cat.

She hated this sort of thing but she had been warned now that she had to behave. Something had happened at Mrs. Willoughby's funeral and she would never be the same again.

Tiny gagged on the watery stew and rice pudding. Alice resolutely locked her out for her own appetite was not good and she did not wish to be discouraged. The beast gorged on the garden's long grass and then slid in through the window and left a pile of matted vomit under her mistress's chair.

She carried the remainder of the food into the garden for the new black stray, which she called The Walrus, because of its curious ingrown whiskers. She waited, shivering, while the kitten devoured the food with threatening noises and elbows stuck up in the air, and then she began the long trek back indoors.

Pausing beneath a sky that was yellow and knotted as a sheep's behind, she was reminded suddenly of chrysanthemums and in the trick of an instant all the confusion of the present deserted her and she was back in that bleak burial maze, looking for Mrs. Willoughby.

It had been a wretched day, cold and bitterly windy. Her tribute of yellow chrysanthemums had struggled against the graveyard wind within their twist of greaseproof paper. Acres of forgotten headstones toppled into dirt, their sinister sentiments blurred by weeds and stones that rattled in the gale; a lost continent, overpopulated and unknown. It was a wonder they had not resorted to high rise.

When she came upon the gathering by the grave she was surprised to see her mother and father standing there. "I'm looking for Mrs. Willoughby," she shouted into the breeze and they beckoned to her. She came closer. It wasn't her mother and father at all, just some other stiff old lady and her little husband. She was disappointed that none of the widow's young men had come along, just relatives, no more interesting than her own. This mild pang was followed by a burst of pure fury. There was a banging on her chest—like the fist of God. One of the women was wearing Mrs. Willoughby's blue suit. Staring at her over the shoulder of the second mourner was the little pointy face of the fox.

"They have stolen her clothes," Alice said aloud and the two women turned to stare. Without consideration, her arm swung out, raising the yellow flowers on their tough wooden stems and she lashed the women's blank faces. Smelly petals rained through the grey day. A pair of spectacles flew into the air and the fox thief's mauve lipstick became corrugated like an alligator's teeth.

The two old men watched in fear, their watery eyes retreating to pin-points of abstraction, knowing that action, whatever it might be, had been left too late and that they would be castigated as fools. One dug into his pocket and produced a pack of wine gums and they each furtively armed themselves with a sweet.

"Lord, she'll have their heads off," one of them remarked, but it was only the helpless little fox that bounced forward from the usurper's shoulders. Alice watched it leaping into the grave, loyal as some trusty pet, and she realised that it was what she herself should have done—flung herself in on top of the box to keep her neighbour company. It was too late now. Her knees had turned to water and with a feeling of great foolishness she thumped on to the gravel.

* * *

The sound of the doorbell summoned her from the garden. She made painful progress to the hall and stood there, the cat's dish in her hand. The doorbell drilled ruthlessly. She crept up to the door and pressed her face against the glass panel. "Who is it?"

"It's us!" cried out the angry voices of Marjorie and Donald's wife, Andrea. They looked so round, so warm, when she at last had let them in. "So good!" Alice remembered her manners.

As they entered she studied their hand-luggage in the hope that they might have brought bread or milk, basic groceries so poignantly luxurious to the housebound. Instead, Andrea offered half a dozen irises with shrivelled lips. Marjorie sniffed grimly around. Her critical eye took in the cold look of the place, the pool of cat sick visible through the kitchen door.

"Have a drink," Alice said. "I think there's sherry. Keep your coats on while I light an electric bar."

"Tea will do."

"There's no milk," she apologised. "I'm confined to quarters."

They followed her into the drawing room where Andrea offered her a photograph of a house. "Ted found it," Andrea said with pride.

Since her accident Alice found it hard to make her brain work. She appeared to exist in some atmosphere heavier than air and the people around her did not seem real.

"Very nice." She stared at the photograph Andrea had given her, wondering what was expected of her. Secretly she thought the house looked like some kind of institution, with skimpy curtains behind the big windows and white paint carelessly slapped on its old grey face. "You deserve it," she added, noting that Andrea's face had not lost its worried look.

There was an uneasy silence and then Andrea said unhappily, "I daresay I do but it will be a long time before I get a chance to rest my bones."

Marjorie looked furious. "She is deliberately playing the fool."

"It's for you, Alice dear," Andrea said. "It's the nursing home. We talked about it at the hospital. Donald went to an awful lot of trouble. It's really very nice."

Alice looked into their agitated middle-aged faces. Middle age was difficult. One was resigned neither to life nor death. The lost opportunities, the accumulated indecisions of half a lifetime, spurred one on to forceful action on the petty matters that remained for disposal. They had been frightened to see her in danger. They had to put her away for safe keeping. It did not occur to them they would be her age in a dozen or so years. Middle age was not a time for identification. Alice remembered it as a time for dismayed absorption in the diminishing self.

"You may put my name down." For a moment they looked guilty but then relief softened their faces. "Put my name down for twenty years from now!"

"Who will want you at eighty-seven?" Marjorie cried out in tactless anger.

"Let me alone, Marjorie." Alice felt very weary.

"She should be in bed, Marge," Andrea whispered. "Look at her."

"Of course she should be in bed," Marjorie replied loudly. "She has had a stroke. She is no longer capable. She is very

100

fortunate not to be in glory with God."

Alice rose hopefully. "I hate to rush you but I am waiting for someone."

"We will wait together," Marjorie was stubborn. "We will stay and welcome your visitor."

Alice nodded. How long before she needed rest so badly that she would agree to be committed to that bleak house where the giant rooms would be festooned with walking frames and prosthetic devices? One would learn to be still in the night for fear of provoking squeaks from the plastic sheeting. There would be no young faces, no animals except those remade as old overcoats; and old faces wrestling with new teeth at plastic-topped tables with a paper napkin tucked in the water glass.

Marjorie stood up and went to the window, whipping back the crumbling lace to demonstrate the emptiness outside. "Who are you expecting?"

She had no one. They all knew it. The doctor had apologised to Donald when he summoned him to her hospital bedside in the middle of the night, when they thought she was going to die. "There's no one else."

"Leave her alone, Marjorie," Andrea urged. "She's confused. She's old."

"I am not old," Alice assured herself. She had been thinking that, if they could not have tea, there might be Marmite or Bovril which they could drink with boiling water. She was hungry and feeling sorry for herself. "People become kings and popes at my age. People take up painting and turn into novelists when they are past sixty. Rich men in their sixties marry girls of eighteen."

All the same, she knew that her sixties were not the same as anyone else's. Circumstances had worn thin the fibre of her life, whereas the popes and lechers were securely knitted into some complicated weave.

Marjorie, on guard at the window, abruptly dropped her

bunch of lace and swooped back into the room. "There is someone out there!"

"She was expecting someone," Andrea said.

Clonk! went the knocker. "I had better go and see ..." Alice's knees cracked with tension as she stood. The children rose and crept behind her to the door.

"What's going on?" Dinah entered like a buffalo.

"Why were you prying at the window?" Alice tried to subdue her happy face.

"I saw you had company. I didn't want to get in the way." Dinah released her hair from a red nylon scarf with threads of lurex.

"Who is this?" Marjorie demanded.

"It's Dinah." Alice allowed herself to smile. The appearance of the black woman was like the sight of Noah to the last wingless animal as the flood foamed over its paws.

She introduced the children.

"You're her family?" Dinah's eyes bulged in disbelief. "I thought you were the welfare. You were bullying her. I saw in the window. I could tell."

"She can't live alone," Marjorie stated.

"I had another spot of bother—a stroke," Alice explained. "They are concerned for my safety."

"She's not alone," Dinah said.

"This is more nonsense." Marjorie's smile was kindly as a chemical spray. "Who else is there?"

"There is me." Dinah beamed menacingly back.

The three of them stared at the black woman in awe.

"She can't afford a housekeeper." Ted's wife prided herself on her plainness of speech.

"She's not my housekeeper," Alice said.

"What, then?"

"It's a special ... arrangement." Alice gave Dinah her begging look.

"It would have to be very special."

"It's special." Dinah switched on some lamps and animated the fire, which the others had forgotten. "I'll make the tea now." She left them staring at one another in the discommoding glow. There was real milk on the tray she brought in, and little buttery biscuits which had formed no part of Alice's store. Alice sipped in humble gratitude. Marjorie was shaping her mouth for interrogation but she was diverted by a huge smile of unsettling innocence. "I am taking religious instruction," Dinah explained. "I had nowhere else to live so madam here agreed to take me in and teach me my prayers, if I would cook and shop and look after her house."

"What kind of religious instruction?" was all Marjorie could say, when she was able to say anything at all.

Dinah unbuttoned a portion of blouse and withdrew a clutch of medals and scapulars. "It's the real thing."

Andrea inspected the holy relics. "I shall have to talk to my husband."

"Yes, ma'am." Dinah flung a bold glance at Alice.

Alice kept quiet until her relatives had left. "Thank you," she said then.

Dinah began to clear the tea things.

"Leave them," Alice coaxed. "There is plenty of time. Sit down and talk to me now."

Dinah set down the tray with a splatter. "I'm not staying. You think I've got nothing better to do?" She watched the struggle of Alice's features, a moth in a web. "I've got a nice room of my own," she said more gently. "I have a job. I've got my own friends."

"What did I do?" Alice whispered.

She shook her head. "It doesn't matter now".

"It's Mrs. Willoughby, isn't it? She was my friend." Alice felt her eyes filling with tears. "Now she's dead. I'm sorry. I did not mean to take you for granted."

"Yes, but you did."

Alice wiped her eyes with a big, bunched-up man's

103

handkerchief, like a cauliflower. "Why did you bother to come back? Why did you defend me in front of the children?"

"I just wanted to see how you were. I never meant to stay. Common sense deserted me when I saw you being pushed around by that Andrex and Margarine."

"Marjorie!" Alice fought a smile. "Don't go, Dinah."

"You give me one good reason."

"Because I need you."

Dinah sniffed and turned away. She seemed to be looking for something in her handbag. Cigarettes and lipstick were flung out on the sofa. At last she brought out a greasy paper bag, seeping steam. She tore the paper and the smell of vinegar made Alice's jaws ache. Dinah brought a chip to her mouth and passed the squashed and scrumptious feast to Alice. "Well, then," she said chewing; "that's all right."

CHAPTER 19

Dinah slept in the room that had belonged to Alice's parents. In the night she got up to look for something warm to wear. She turned the key in a mahogany wardrobe heaving with ornament. Ghosts flew out of the brittle suits and wilting dresses. She turned on the light and inspected the puritan moulds of Mother's shoes, a silk dressing gown reeking of camphor. Wrapping herself in the gown she moved to the dressing table and studied a wedding picture in a silver frame; the man's arms curving like bananas out of a too-tight jacket, the woman in white, stiff as a lily, her look as challenging as the general of an opposing army. Poor little Alice.

She fetched her cigarettes and some matches, lit one and dropped the burning match into an ashtray. Before it had time to die she pulled a strand of silk from the dressing gown and put it in the ashtray with a little bit of the wedding picture whittled out of its frame. She watched them burn and then she turned her attention back to the wardrobe and rooted until she found a fawn cardigan which she put on over the dressing gown, and a pair of men's socks. She climbed back under the cold quilt. Blooming freezing! "What a way to spend my night off," she grumbled.

The clocks chimed. Alice lay rigid in the bed, waiting. For once they failed to send her hurtling back to childhood. She listened to their odd cries and complaints and entertained a bold notion. *I need never wind them again if I don't want to.* Oh, the Lord save us, such a terrible thing. And she didn't care.

Dinah's snores rumbled amid the relics. She had the power

105

to subdue ghosts, to disperse the clinging dust of their determination. The thought of her in the next room was comforting and disturbing. "I won't be able to sleep," she fretted. "Oh, Mama, Papa, I'm sorry this is the best I can do but at least I won't be bullied any more. Or will I? Oh, Sacred Heart of Jesus, I place all my trust in Thee. In the meantime, I'll lie awake on nails." In a minute she drifted off to sleep, exhausted by anticipation.

In the morning, she awoke early. She tiptoed to Dinah's room. She wanted to look at her sleeping, to see if there was any trace left of the baby she had paid for.

She turned the door handle and crept into the camphor-smelling mausoleum. She stood there, dithery with dismay. She stared at the black figure on the bed, who paused in the act of washing her behind to stare back at Alice. It was Tiny, taking advantage of the warm spot bequeathed by Dinah's sleeping body. Dinah was gone.

She searched the room, everywhere, even under the bed. Tiny the cat followed, swaggering her rump as if she knew what Alice did not. "Dinah!" Alice called out on a little sigh, but she knew she was not in the house.

Had she been unsettled by the clocks? Had she lain awake in the night doubting a future spent with a dull older woman? Alice put on the kettle for breakfast and fed the cat. She slung a coat over her nightwear and went outside with the milk-bottle to leave something for the new stray.

A dead morning; branches silvered like the lead of pencils against a blackening sky. The leaves on the ground had gone brown and soft, then hardened up again like shrunken skulls. She put the saucer on the ground and stood up with a shudder for poor, dainty Mrs. Willoughby going soft beneath the ground. Not wanting to, she glanced over at her neighbour's window, and was shocked to see that the house looked not merely dark but derelict. She frowned at this, her lips working at some silent reassurance, until she realised that the pretty curtains had been taken from the windows.

Something startled her. A noise of battle deep in the jungle of the garden. A thing shot into the sky out of the bushes, something spiky and hairy and *alive*—for it was flailing for purchase. It landed at her feet and spat at her slippered toes.

"Kitty!" she cried, relieved by the familiar sight of The Walrus but uneasy about the velocity of its flight.

Another shape appeared. Alice picked up a stone, just for show, but when the bushes were sundered it was Dinah who emerged, her head and shoulders strewn with dead leaves and cobwebs. "Oh, thank heavens," Alice murmured. Dinah's skin gleamed. Her breath came out in frosty puffs. How much better than beige-skinned people she looked in this grey climate! Already Alice found she was regarding her with parental pride. "I knew you'd be here." Alice told a lie. "I came out to wait so we could have breakfast together." She touched Dinah's wrist and felt, beneath the chilled surface of her skin, pulsing blood. She took her hand away quickly. It was a long time since she had touched another person's skin.

"Do you know what's in there?" Dinah's tone was accusing.

Alice shook her head warily.

"There's a garden."

"A jungle, more like."

"I love a garden," Dinah said.

"Well, it's too much for me."

"Not for me. All my life I wanted a garden. I never had more than a window box high up in the sky where the wind broke that which the frost did not bite."

"In the sky?" Alice looked bewildered.

"There are fruit trees in there," Dinah said. "There would be flowers if they could get some light. How come they got planted if it was too much for you?"

"It was my father's garden."

"What was it like?" She inspected the muddy scratches on her hands and then turned eager eyes on Alice. She under-

107

stood nothing of polite enquiry. If she asked a question it was because she wanted to know.

"I never knew the names of most of the flowers," Alice said. "I saw it in the way a child sees these things."

Quite suddenly she saw it: a square of perfect lawn with one swirling metal seat and wooden markers poised around the verges, as if for somersault. A twisting path of crazy paving, winking with pastilles of glass called cats' eyes, led to the orchard where summer trees spat fruit on the ground with a whispery thump: rosy knuckled apples, paunchy plums, pears squat as frogs. Inside the fruit worms hollowed out grottoes and wasps simmered on their surface. The soft fruits seemed themselves like insects: close to the earth, livid and lumbering, a colony of loganberries. On sparse shrubs with thorns that were almost horns, hairy gooseberries grew, full of seeds and light. Flowers everywhere, dressed up in all their colours like people on a parade.

"I'm not much for describing things," she apologised.

"I'll get it tidied up," Dinah promised. Her toe poked restlessly at the kitten which made snarling sorties at the milk.

"Leave it alone," Alice sharply rebuked. "It is a poor homeless creature and it is hungry."

"Cats are randy scavengers. You are a sentimental old woman."

"Take care, Dinah," Alice warned. "Do not deride emotion. In the civilised world it is natural to nurture defenceless things. You have become too independent. Perhaps if you yourself owned an animal—or had a child ... Oh, bless us, sorry, sorry!" She fled into a blizzard of mumbles, remembering. "I'll make the tea."

Dinah worked in the garden all morning. Alice washed the breakfast dishes and made the beds. As she was smoothing her quilt she got the odd notion that she would like to be beneath it so she climbed in and fell fast asleep. She woke at lunchtime. She felt tremendous. The heaviness and the pain and worry seemed to have seeped out of her with that sleep. She made a lunch of beans and toast, her heart lurching with pleasure as she set two places. After she had called Dinah she grew anxious. Would the girl still be cool with her?

Dinah stamped in, beating mud off her boots and sending plumes of frosty air into the cold kitchen.

"Horseshit!" she scowled.

"What? Oh ...!"

"That's what my garden needs. Proper steaming horseshit. No quarter pounds of chemical fertiliser on my patch." She scooped her beans and shook a fork at Alice. "You know what else? We're going to get this house warm. You may be already half dead but my blood is not yet ambient to the morgue. I want more coal and electric fires in every room. I almost died in my bed of cold last night."

"That will cost," Alice said.

"Just say now if it's too large a price." Dinah's look held no challenge. She only wanted to know.

"No." Alice was ashamed. "And I'm sorry, Dinah, for so tactlessly forgetting about the baby."

"Oh, it's okay. If we are to believe what we are told, he is in heaven now, wearing his crown. Or perhaps, because he was so small, it would only be half a crown."

"Half a crown. That's what I paid for you."

Dinah grabbed Tiny by her scruff and tormented her, tweaking her helpless toes. Alice was about to intercede but she looked at her beans, opting for discretion. The cat, inexplicably, shrilled with delight and Dinah gave her great big laugh.

In the afternoon they walked together to the shops and bought food for two, which is an adventure, whereas shopping for one is an expense. Dinah liked tomato sauce and Mr. Kipling's cakes and individual trifles and sweet sherry and potato crisps. She shopped as if for a party. Alice tried

109

to introduce a pack of All-Bran to their basket, for, like most people nowadays, she confused fibrous food with moral fibre and felt guilty about eating the zesty, easy things with their artificial flavourings.

Dinah put the cereal back on the shelf. "It's tension makes the bowels seize up and that kind of stuff makes me tense," she said firmly.

"Look at those!" She pointed in the window of a garden shop where giant boxes of spring bulbs were displayed. Alice tried to think of something sensible. The tulips on the box were too big and too red, the bluebells a jangle of blue against the cheap yellow frills of daffodil. The picture fitted exactly into some frame of memory. She could even see into the centre of those tulips, from whose dark, lacquered floor sprang exotic, powdery antennae. "I daresay it's a swizz," she said wistfully.

"Only two pounds ninety, though."

"We could splurge."

It cost a bit more for Dinah took two packs of bulbs and some smaller boxes which promised snowdrops and crocuses and lily of the valley and in spite of her resolution she added a costly sack of peat compound. Alice found herself counting out twenty pounds and the change was in coins.

She was quiet on the way back, worrying and disapproving. Dinah was thoughtful too but hers was the silence of effort for the bag of fertiliser was heavy as a dead sheep.

When they got home Dinah wanted to show off her work on the garden but Alice shook her head stiffly and sank into a chair.

"Ah, you're tired." Dinah fetched a rug from the bedroom and wrapped it around her knees. She tested cushions as if they were plums and found one that was plump and soft to ease under the offended eggshell skull. She rattled out the fire until she had a decent blaze and then on top of that she brought the electric fire from the drawing room and switched it on—two bars.

"Dear child!" Alice remained rigid within her comfortable cocoon. "I am loath to make an issue. There is not money to burn."

"Nor chances to be taken! You have been ill and suffered shock. You have to keep warm!" Defiantly, Dinah flung a log on the fire. "For what are you hoarding your money? There are no pockets in the shroud."

"The children believe I am not capable of looking after my resources."

"Oh, it's Margarine, is it? Well, you tell her this has nothing to do with your resources. I have a good job washing dishes in a café at night. I will pay my share."

"You work at night?" Peevish anxiety buzzed about her. "I'll be alone"

"You'll be all right. I come home at four in the morning and I'll go straight to bed. Don't answer the door to anyone. You'll hear me come in and you'll know it's all right."

Alice felt her eyelids sinking. "You mustn't spoil me, Dinah."

Dinah stroked her gently on the hair—the searing, compromising touch of sympathy. "It is my belief that more people are spoilt by cruelty than kindness. Now close your eyes and rest."

"All right then, just for a minute." It was lovely to feel the heat of the fire seeping through the soft rug to her legs.

When she opened her eyes she thought she was dreaming. The room had been transformed. Instead of the gaunt yellow light dripping down the walls there were gentle pools of radiance at elbow level. The curtains had been pulled, shutting out the gnashing wind. It reminded her of Mrs. Willoughby's window when she had spied on it from her scullery.

"What have you done?" Her head bobbed fearfully about for Dinah.

111

"I brought the little lamps down from the drawing room. Nobody goes in there except visitors. We might as well have the place nice for ourselves instead of Margarine and the welfare."

"I don't like moving things around," Alice fretted. 'They've always been there, since Mama and Papa's day."

"Your mama and papa would probably have liked the whole world kept the same, but it hasn't happened."

Alice's toes did an involuntary stretch and quiver beneath the rug, the way Tiny's sometimes did.

Before she went back outside to plant her new bulbs, Dinah sat in a chair opposite to admire her handiwork. Her short leather skirt had risen and she wore popsox. Her knees gleamed like the heads of elder statesmen.

Later, when she had been pleasantly woken by tea, Alice agreed to a tour of the garden. Cautiously, she crept through the entry Dinah had hacked in the undergrowth, stepping onto what had once been the lawn, and shone her torch down on the resurrected borders where labels named the tulips and crocuses and bluebells which the newly-planted, bad-looking onions might become. Smeared with frost in the smoky light, the white labels stuck up like gravestones in a miniature cemetery. She voiced this thought, and then could have bitten off her tongue.

Dinah only laughed. "Maybe I am some kind of grave-digger. Maybe I was sent here to dig up your past."

CHAPTER 20

On her way to the kitchen in the morning, Alice stopped to look in on Dinah—not wake her, just look.

She had heard her coming in at four with a soft giggle and a "shhh!" admonition to herself.

"She's been drinking!" Alice thought, critical at first, but she reminded heself that the girl had been out until all hours in all sorts of weather.

She had her hand on the knob when the door opened of its own accord and a man walked out. He was small and foreign, possibly Armenian. He wore a pair of striped underpants and a hat. "Boy, what a nice country you have here—marvellous girls," he said in his accented voice. His smile was so friendly beneath his small, sad eyes that Alice involuntarily smiled back.

For a time the surprise was so great—like seeing the often-imagined bogeyman of childhood actually crawling out of the cupboard—that Alice did nothing. She imagined the smile still clung. The man walked along the passage on jaunty, knotted legs and let himself into the bathroom. She dodged out of the way to avoid his whistling return and fled down to the kitchen. "Coffee!" She prompted her brain and occupied her fluttering hands with beans and boiling water.

Then she couldn't drink it. She wanted to hush its snaking fragrance lest it transmit invitation. Sure enough, in walked Dinah, in night attire, her arm around the old foreign gentle-man who was somewhat covered in a silk dressing gown. At first Alice was so occupied with her ordinary affront that she failed to recognise the garment. Father's silk dressing gown!

He had bought it many years ago on a trip to Paris and had worn it until it had a smell. Alice had to stuff it with mothballs before she could face it after his death.

"Coffee smells good," Dinah said.

"What is this?" Alice's voice emerged, ratty and shaken. "Why is he wearing father's dressing gown?"

"Because he has no clothes on underneath," Dinah laughed. "He has been hard at work to keep me warm in that arctic ghost-box."

"Filthy!" Alice squeezed her eyes shut. "In my parents' bedroom."

"There's no harm." Dinah playfully pushed at Alice's knee. She filled three coffee cups and handed them around. "Tell me, where's the harm?"

"Get that ... creature out of here."

"He is God's creature."

Alice looked away. "Out! You have no more morals than the cat."

"You seem fond enough of cats." She sat with knees splayed.

The man put down his coffee cup and turned upon Alice his intent, kind, monkey gaze. "Forgive me," he said.

"It's unpardonable."

"Yes." He looked away and she was glad. "You are lonely. I have offended your sense of order. I understand. I too am lonely." He disturbed her once more with his benign look. "I am so lonely that I record women's voices in public places and when I am at home I leave them playing in an empty room so that I can pretend it is a wife and a mother-in-law discussing me."

He left to go to the bedroom and get dressed. He did not come back to the kitchen. Alice heard Dinah saying goodbye to him. Watching his unfinished coffee, she felt an unfair discomfort.

Dinah came back and slapped a five pound note on the

table. "He left that to pay for the dry cleaning of your father's dressing gown." She sat down, drinking her coffee. "Well, are you happy?"

"I have never been so upset in my life."

"Lucky old you, then."

"I must speak my mind since I can see you have no shame. You are a trollop, Dinah. This house has never known such carry-on."

"How did you get born?"

"I was born out of a holy, wedded union."

"They still did it the same way, you know. Anyway, who do you think thought up this dirty business in the first place?"

"I think, Dinah, it would be better if you went to your room."

"God did!"

"Why do you want to upset me?"

"Because you upset my friend. He was a nice poor man who was dying for want of human touch. See, Alice, we all need that."

Alice shuddered. She turned her bleak, needy eye on Dinah and Dinah couldn't help herself, she had to come and put her arms around her. She wanted that—warm, solid arms; but she could not escape the notion that the same arms had come warm from sinful embraces. It made her think of what Dinah and the man had done together. Animals! She imagined she could smell him on her. Yes, she could. It was the same smell that had been in father's dressing gown! Oh, horror! Danger and the mocking mirth of experience lurched over the edges of every comfort. She felt she was held in the grip of evil, snug against Dinah's breast. She broke away, thumping upon Dinah's chest with her fist, her face screwed up so that her bottom teeth showed like a pekinese dog. "Get off me! Get away!"

Dinah backed off. Her lip stuck out with its stubborn, angry look. "You could have never had a child. It would have frozen to death. You are like this house, ice to the foundation."

"Sticks and stones," Alice shrugged, although the words cut deeply. "I promised I would take you on!"

"You said you needed me."

"Yes, well, I didn't know you then. I will not go back on my word. I can see I shall have my work cut out."

"What are you going to do? Beat my backside?"

"We will leave your backside out of it. We will follow a course which you yourself prescribed, when you were lying to my nephews' wives." She imposed upon Dinah a face that was weighted down with Old Values. "I shall see to your prayers."

"I should have let them slam you in the old folk's home."

"God moves in mysterious ways. You will learn to be a decent woman, Dinah. You will spend the day in your room, please, reading the Good Book."

"Oh, no! I'm off to the garden."

"You will do as I say."

"And who are you to say?"

"I am ... your mother."

"Say it again."

"... your mother."

"Say it and kiss me."

'Yes ... No!"

Anyway she was glad to go back to her room. Sleep had been sketchy and she was yawning again. It was still warm in the bed and she climbed in, hoisting the blankets up around her.

Alice disapproved when she came in with her copy of scripture. A good woman should be fully dressed to read the word of the Lord. There was another *frisson* of aversion when she saw that Dinah was already clutching her own version of scripture, which had been authorised not by Jesus Christ but by a king of England. Her lips gathered reproach but she decided it was a challenge best met by indifference. "I want you to read out loud so I shall know you are not shirking," she said. "I shall expect to hear you."

Dinah scanned the book idly, as if it was a thriller. "Abraham begat Isaac; and Isaac begat Jacob and Jacob begat Judas and his brethren," she sleepily commenced.

Alice closed the door and listened outside it. "And Judas begat Phares and Zara of Thamar; and Phares begat Esrom; and Esrom begat Aram ... " her voice drowsily trailed away.

"Go on!" Alice thumped on the door.

"And Aram begat A-min-a-dab!" Dinah deliberately emphasised Aram's most peculiar choice of name for his son and then she came to a full stop.

"And?" Alice pursued her through the keyhole.

"And they enjoyed it!" Dinah shouted back.

CHAPTER 21

"A viper at the bosom," Alice muttered as she shook out mats and poked the hose of the hoover into old settled colonies of dust and vermin. From her parents' bedroom the begettings proceeded interminably. She suffered pangs for the good old days of serious cleanliness; the lye for scrubbing, the castor oil for bodily purging and weekly confessions for turning out the soiled spirit.

Priests found out a lot in confession. A bad girl, Brigid Mulvey, startlingly told her so at school. They were curious too. Where did he touch you? With *what*?

How could such things occur? She paused, the vacuum cleaner droning. Had the man accosted Dinah in the street or had he followed her home? How did he convey his intention? Why had he taken off *all* his clothes? Naturally no such thing had ever happened to her. But *why*?

Passing Dinah's door she banged on it with the nozzle of the hoover and Dinah read out in her sweet, low voice: "The light of the body is in the eye; if therefore thine eye be single, thy whole body shall be full of light. But if thine eye be evil, thy whole body shall be full of darkness. If therefore the light that is in thee be darkness, how great is that darkness."

She went into the drawing room and looked at the mirror. Her eyes looked back at her, dull as raisins.

No light! It wasn't her fault. She had always been good. It was the way God had made her, the way her life had shaped her.

"I want the light!" she said.

"Open your eyes and look around," said a voice inside her.

"My eye is single!" she protested.

The suction contraption moaned and moaned.

She wound the clocks, pulling on their chains as if drawing noxious entrails. She had not bothered to wind them yesterday. Now it seemed that this neglect had preceded a general collapse of standards.

When she was exhausted by her effort, the house seemed no cleaner than before. The weather, of course, was not up to much. The light that seeped into the porch and through the fanlight was grey and actually seemed to darken the hall. *How great was that darkness.* The odd thing was ... Her mind fuddled off in that peculiar way it repeatedly did since she had had her accident. The odd thing was, the hall always seemed to contain this dark light, no matter what the outside weather.

The odd thing was ... the man had seemed nice.

One could not judge men, not in the same way as women. It was a well-known fact that men had poor control in these matters. To whom was it known? And how?

She missed Dinah.

She lit the fire and drank tea close to midget flames that gave no warmth. In spite of her efforts the place was not comfortable. She wasn't a homemaker. Was it possible to make a home for one? The questions of years were heaped up around the place, unused, like gadgets with broken parts.

She missed Dinah.

She had intended to leave her in her room until tea but in the end Christian charity prevailed and she summoned her for lunch. She set out the flowery china bowls and faintly soggy linen napkins for a good example and then she sat down quivering with excitement, with the pleasurable forgiveness of saints.

Dinah came wearing father's old cardigan over her nightie

and a pair of his socks on her feet. At once Alice's agreeable feelings diminished. She did not even pause to wash her hands but instead moved around the room and, with a critical sigh, switched on the lamps. The room bloomed. "Ah, yes." Alice handed her a glass of sherry, feeling crushed.

Dinah gazed sleepily into the fire and tasted her drink. Alice admired the smooth beauty of her skin, burnished by firelight. She looked dreamy, unrepentant. Perhaps its just a phase, she thought.

"Your friend!" She made her voice pleasant and busied her spoon with soup. "What is his name?"

Dinah shrugged. "I don't know."

Dismay flared in her again. She took a calming drop of sherry. "Where did you meet him?"

"He came up to me in a public house." Dinah dabbled bread in her soup. "He told me he was lonely and wanted to sleep with me. He asked for my address."

"You gave him my address!" Her voice sharpened on an edge of anger. She could not help herself. "Am I to expect strange men to come pounding on the door throughout the dead hours of the night?"

"I gave him the address of the café where I work. He came there to look for me. He looked so hungry and so sad that I gave him his supper and took him home." She looked into Alice's shocked and eager eyes. "I am not sorry. I cannot say that I am when I am not. I was kind to him. He kept me warm. If I am to be damned then I would rather be in hell with the likes of him than in paradise with the vinegary and the virtuous. He was not an uncaring man."

"No," Alice had to agree. "All the same, lust is a deadly sin. We are each of us the guardian of a soul. Eat your soup, dear."

Dinah chewed her seeping bread with relish. "It seems to me a lot of people are too selfish about their souls." She paused to break the rest of her bread into the bowl. Alice itched to stop her. "It makes me think of a little girl with a blue dress which the nuns gave her and, when she had it on, she couldn't play with her brothers and sisters or help her mother in their hut for fear of getting dirty.

"In the same way, we cannot stoop to love one another in case we might muddy our souls. We live in this dirty world. We were put here by God, who made it."

Alice had an uncomfortable memory of herself standing stiffly on the edge of the garden while her father played in the mud. "We are not talking now of innocent children," she said. "We are speaking of adults with free will and the ability to rein it. We are speaking—I will use the word again—of lust."

"Yes, well, why not?" Dinah upturned to Alice her bright face, faintly moustached with tomato soup. How did she manage to look so innocent? "Tell me, what does that word mean to you?"

Alice heaped soup into her mouth. "You know I have no experience of that side of life. Lust is sinful."

"Sin is not your department."

"I know, but you are in my care. I feel responsible."

"All right, then. I'll make you a promise. I will go to a priest and confess my so-called sin if you will answer my question in terms of feeling and belief."

"We were not brought up to speak of such things," Alice's eager eye betrayed her heavy tone.

"Yes, but you are quick enough to do so when it is none of your business. Just tell me what you think."

"It's an appetite," Alice said reluctantly. "There's some kind of a thrill."

"That's right, and it's rude, isn't it—tits and pricks and all sorts of unspeakable stuff."

"Stop it!"

"All right. I just wanted to get that said. That is the image we all have, even after we lose our innocence. The reality is the endless trudge of people looking for love, or just for someone to accept them. Do you ever think about sex?"

Alice shook her head as if eager to part it from her body, but then she said: "Ye-es."

"I am glad to hear it. The impulse of creation is closely allied to the spirit. I have always believed that those who are indifferent to sex are poorly endowed with spirit."

"You're tying me up, Dinah. I don't think of it in that way."

"You never get a pain of longing?"

"Only in my heart."

"That's the real thing. That's where it starts. Have you ever read anything about sex?"

Again the shameful pause. Alice stared into her soup and its worried surface wrinkled and dulled. "Everything I could get my hands on."

"Me too," Dinah said. "Like all the experts they tell you everything except the thing you need to know. It is an attempt to join another person. It is the yearning for belonging. All the loneliness gone—all the burden of bearing oneself; only for a few little minutes, but even so."

"I never thought of that."

"How could one think of such a thing?"

They were quiet. After a long pause in which the soup transmuted its surface into a sheeny red leatherette, like the covering on the café booths, Dinah became aware that Alice was brewing curiosity.

"Yes?"

"I was wondering ... " Embarrassment flooded her cheeks with youth, but she pressed on: "Was it ... like that ... with your foreign gentleman?"

Dinah laughed softly. "Bless us, no. That was a more mundane transaction, a recognised exchange between all losers and a great many married couples. He kept my feet warm and gave me a laugh."

Alice's eye flickered away and her mouth tightened. Hell's bells, Dinah thought.

"You have no standards, no civilised standards! Why, you did not even bother to wash your hands before sitting down to lunch."

Dinah inspected her surprising pink palms. "You may be right. Would you like me to go on with my reading, then?"

"Carry on." Alice located and put on her glasses as if it was she who was about to read.

Dinah picked up her copy of testament and allowed the pages to splay, apparently at random. "For out of the heart proceed evil thoughts, murders, adulteries, fornications, thefts, false witness, blasphemies; these are the things which defile a man: but to eat with unwashed hands defileth not a man."

Alice was furious. "Don't be smart, miss. In any case you have damned yourself! The Lord's own words! Fornications . . . defileth a man!"

Dinah pondered this. She closed the book and poised it winningly beneath her chin. "Fornication," she mused. "That's a mighty big word. Fornication, I would think, would be a sport of philanderers. I never did anything but a bit of screwing around."

Alice fell back in a disarray of doubt. "Well, don't do it again," she said lamely.

"Listen, you know something?" Dinah leaned forward, irresistibly confiding. "I have other friends, fully clothed. How would you like it if I brought them here to meet you?"

Alice quailed. "If you wish. Bring your friends, do. Bring them for Christmas."

"You know something else? You have beautiful china."

She held up the flowery bowl, still with its congealing content. "If it was not for the soup, you could see right through it."

"My mother's china!" Alice was surprised by a glow of

123

warmth, reputedly the reward of the home-maker. "I put it out for you. You are to have every advantage. You can have a bath if you want," she added recklessly. "The water is scalding."

"Well, fancy! I will take advantage, but first I must do some work on my garden."

"Let me come with you!" Alice eagerly stood.

"No, it's too cold. You have to stay by the fire."

Dinah went off to put on some clothes and Alice did the dishes, intrigued by the warm water gushing from the taps, dispersing gelid soup and sticky sherry. What luxury!

She was putting away her good plates when she saw Father striding past the scullery window in the dusk. Her heart gave a warning thump and she clutched at it, almost dropping a piece of china. She squinted at the pane. Teasing, it flung back a picture of her ugly scullery. Now she could make out the ghost again and she saw with astonishment that death had adorned his bald pate with a fine crop of black curls. But of course it was Dinah, sensibly kitted out in Father's old gardening clothes which were preserved, along with everything else, in the giant wardrobe. All the same it gave her a pang to think that here she was, sixty years on, excluded from mucky play, just as when it really had been Father and she was seven and all her life's work was keeping clean.

"No more!" she growled and slapped a tear off her jowl. "I want some fun."

* * *

Dinah stopped digging and frowned out of the gloom. She smelled smoke. She sniffed and turned around and there was Alice with a look of determination and a box of matches in her hands. She had started a blaze in the pile of dead wood and weed that Dinah had cut away from the garden.

"What are you doing?" Dinah stood with her boot on her spade. "I told you to stay by the fire."

"Ah, but I am by the fire," Alice said. "Somebody has to clear up all this mess you're making."

Dinah came and stood beside her. "It's beautiful. Everyone should make their fires under the sky." She gave Alice a friendly squeeze. "You're a tough old boot, that's for sure. I think I have finally met my match."

"It's called a bonfire!" Alice joyfully educated. "It's traditional. We used to have them on Hallowe'en and Guy Fawkes. All the children would gather round and roast sausages and marshmallows on sticks."

"You did that?" Dinah demanded. "You and your parents and your brother and perhaps some neighbouring children, all screaming and singing around this big fire and roasting sausages on sticks?"

"Not us. It was done."

"Not you." Dinah was thoughtful. "Tell me about yourself, growing up."

"There's nothing to tell." Alice struggled against the other woman's directness. "I've had a quiet life."

"That doesn't matter. Tell me the first thing that comes to mind. Anything you can remember."

To please Dinah she made an effort. She poked the fire with a long, twisted branch of applewood as an *aide-mémoire*. "I remember a glass porch veiled by spiders. There was a wicker chair with pieces that stuck out, harsh as toenails. A cushion, velvet, the colour of blood, one corner worn black and bald as a teddy bear's nose. There was a shelf with potted plants which always had a faded look because the porch didn't get much sun. Lower down was another shelf, meant for books. It housed an untidy array of periodicals, which were about prayer—or insurance.

125

"There was a single volume bound in green and preserved in dust—a Child's Dickens. I used to wonder what that was— a child's dickens—but I never actually opened the book."

"That's not a mental excavation of any magnitude," Dinah scoffed. "The porch looks now exactly as you have described it."

"I suppose it does." Alice looked surprised. "I haven't noticed it for years.

"I have changed nothing—yet everything is changed by the loss of my dear parents. They were the salt of the earth— not like young people nowadays, gallivanting with the first person who takes their fancy. The marrieds are no better. First hint of a rough wind and it's all talk of divorce."

"Your parents . . . " Dinah prompted.

"They had a wonderful marriage. They stuck together through thick and thin. Why, I remember . . . " Her face abruptly lost its animation and she fell silent.

"That's enough old talk, now," Dinah said quickly. "Have we got any sausages?"

"Sausages? We just had lunch."

"All the same we have to have sausages if this is a bonfire. You said so."

"They'll be horrible. Oh, never mind. Right-o!"

She fetched the sausages and a tin plate and plucked a brass toasting fork from the wall. On her way out, she tucked the sherry bottle under her arm.

The fire had subsided. Dinah found more branches to put on top but they only smouldered over the bed of rosy, crackling ashes. She took the sausage that Alice handed her, gored and squashed by the long fork, and squatted over the bleaching fingerbones of twig. Fat seeped into the fire and a luscious, fatty scent crept back up on the woodsmoke.

"It is nice," Alice admitted and she passed Dinah the sherry. The other, praising this improvisation, lifted the bottle to her lips. "Now all we need is the music."

126

"I don't think the neighbours would appreciate a campfire jamboree," Alice chortled uneasily.

"It's all right. What I had in mind was a song from your father."

"Put on a record, you mean? We'd never hear it."

"Open the window. Don't leave him out of the fun."

"He did like fun," Alice had to agree.

She found a record of "Mother Machree", a particular favourite of his once upon a time. She applied it to the old-fashioned machine, daunting now only in its assortment of knobs. She would laugh at this moment, if anyone said it looked like a coffin.

When she opened the kitchen window to let out the sound, she did not immediately rejoin Dinah, but stood there, spying on the view. Strange to see the garden coming to life again, its peculiar little paths once more full of promise. The figure poking at the fire, the frail, damaged tenor voice floating out over smoke and woodspark, made her feel that her father was very close to her. She was at peace. Oddly, after the awful grief at the funeral, she did not miss Mrs. Willoughby. She felt her absence, but only as if she had gone on holiday and they were soon to meet again.

Of course she had Dinah to keep her on her toes. Father would have liked Dinah. They might even have sung together. When she thought of this she imagined she heard an earthy echo of father's infirm tone. There *was* a second voice. Dinah was singing with her Father. She crept outside and sat quietly on the old garden bench to listen.

Dinah took a sausage off the fork and fed it to her waiting audience, Tiny, Alice's cat and the small stray she had named The Walrus.

"Where did you learn that song?" Alice called out of the dark.

"From a friend." She blew on a sausage to cool it. The cats

tottered on their hind legs and pawed the air in imprecation. "We might have musical evenings."

"Why are you feeding the cats? I thought you hated cats."

"Come here where I can see you. I am using the cats as testers. If they fall down with their paws in the air we will dine elsewhere."

Alice stayed where she was, unable to decide if Dinah was making fun of her. In due course Dinah came and joined her, offering a plate of freshly burnt food. The wind blew gusts of warmth at them from the embers of the fire and through the open window of the house the lamps showed golden and inviting. Alice took a sausage in her fingers. "So this it it!" she murmured. "What?" Dinah said, passing the sherry bottle. Alice swigged like a vagrant and passed the apéritif back. Contentment, she thought. So this is contentment!

CHAPTER 22

"Bless me, Father, for I have sinned."

For some reason, Dinah actually did go to confession.

She pulled back purple curtains to see what kind of man she was to confide in and saw red jowls and frightened blue eyes. Perhaps he was afraid of the dark. The penitential drapes smelled of dust. The priest caught her looking at him and covered the side of his face with his hand.

"It is thirty years," she said, "since my last confession."

"How have you sinned, my child?"

"Oh, Lord knows, I could write a book. Fornication?"

"On one occasion or on a number of occasions?"

"Not a whole lot, now you come to mention it."

"Did you take pleasure?"

"Where there was any to be taken. Why do you ask such a thing?"

"Are you truly sorry for your sins?"

"I don't know. I have yet to meet a person who was not more sorry at the end of their days, for lost opportunity than for lost virtue."

"Well, try to be good in future. Your sins are forgiven. For your penance ... "

"Wait a minute!" The wood creaked as Dinah's knees shifted in annoyance. "You are not forgiving my sins. You are dismissing them. It is true that all this is of no account in the large scheme of the earth's decline, but even so. You don't really care, do you, if I end up in hell or Havana?"

"Patience, child," he urged, and a slice of startled blue appeared between his fingers, like the sky viewed between skyscraper rooflines. "We are simply trying to keep up with the times. There isn't much demand for this service any more. Confession is no longer a draw. Mass absolution is the thing. All I get in here nowadays are old ladies who like the dark and someone to talk to. I haven't had a fornication in, oh, a decade."

"Ah," Dinah said. "It is a part of the materialistic revolution—the refusal to believe in God. Even the Church has become a conspirator. We will have to work this out for ourselves. You asked if I took pleasure. I'll make a bargain. I will fill you in on the nature of carnal bliss if you, as holy man and celibate, will exchange your experiences of mystical ecstacy."

"Get out of that!" the priest snarled in embarrassment. "Do you want absolution or not?"

Dinah thought about it. "Confession was what I really wanted—an opportunity to discuss my imperfections. And you did ask if I took pleasure."

The holy man sighed most mournfully. "I have had little consolation. I read the lives of the saints with envy. The most I have experienced are fleeting feelings of happiness in the certainty of God. The rest of the time I live in doubt."

"There you are!" Dinah paused to light two cigarettes and she poked one in through the wire grille to her new acquaintance. "It is much the same for me with my fornications—occasional brief bliss but most of the time a feeling of 'what-the-hell-am-I-doing-here?' This is most interesting. Now let us move on to the nature of forgiveness. Do you really believe that you can forgive sins? If you have such power then why, if I come in to you and say, 'I owe ten thousand pounds,' can you not say, 'Your debts are forgiven you'? The sin cannot be undone even if you are truly sorry. The transgression must remain outstanding just as the debt would be."

"Ah, yes," the priest said, livening; "but there is a penance attached to the forgiveness of sin. If you owed a debt I would tell you to pay. So I ask you to pay for your sins by performing a penance—which I was about to do before you interrupted me."

"I am sorry, Father. Pass on to the penance."

"Your sins are forgiven." He blessed her with fingers too soft for a man's hand. "For your penance say five decades of the rosary."

He began to mutter the ancient formula of expiation.

"Excuse me, please!" Dinah interrupted again.

"Yes?" When he frowned, his smooth face was marked all over by the years of doubt and compromise, like paw prints on clean lino.

"If prayer was given to us as a means of consolation, a manner of conversing with our heavenly mother and father, why is it also employed as penance?"

"Oh, good God!" he appealed. "What do I know? Perhaps the theory is the same as that which argues against the imprisonment of criminals. Maybe it is seen as a means of positive reform rather than punishment."

"That is fairly satisfactory," Dinah nodded. "You are an interesting man, you know. Perhaps I will commit some small sin in the near future so that we may take up this conversation again."

Dinah did not immediately leave the stifling box but rummaged in her handbag and then thrust a gurgling bag around her door and through the windowed front of the booth.

"What are you doing?" The priest defended himself nervously.

"It's a present. I brought you a bottle of whiskey."

"Oh, no. I couldn't take it." In the gloom she could perceive that his eye was already trying to identify, through brown paper, the brand and nationality of the refreshment.

"It's a ten-year-old Irish," she enlightened him. "Where I

originate, a man might throw out his daughter if she committed a transgression that was called deadly—oh, poisoning her husband, perhaps. But you have been clement to me and, although I do not believe that a magic word can quite erase sin, all the same I am surprised by how new I feel. Please honour me by accepting my gift."

He took the whiskey. "Come and talk to me again. Come even if you haven't a sin. It's dull in here and I enjoyed your company."

"Yes, I would like that." She hesitated and then she said: "I have a favour to ask of you. Would you say a prayer for a little old lady who called me her daughter? She is of no account and yet in a strange way I believe it was her influence that brought me here. In fact, you might say she has changed my life."

"She sounds a remarkable woman." For the first time the priest smiled and Dinah saw a handsome face which might have charmed out of a different kind of dark and she felt a deep compassion for his bondage to God's holy order.

"She is, in fact, a kind of miracle." She grinned at him mischievously. "She is pure white."

"Well, now." God's representative looked nervous again. "That's not so unusual these days."

"And she is a virgin."

CHAPTER 23

Whenever Dinah handed a gentleman friend his hat, she commanded him to go forth and tell no man but, as is the way with miracles and chance encounters, he would spread the word far and wide. People came from all parts to seek this woman who, it was said, was nice and wanted nothing, was kind, but did not seek ransoms of thankfulness.

Several days after her confession, when the zeal had worn off but a heavy workload kept her in the state of grace, she was interested to note a new crowd in the café, not the usual huddled masses but an assortment of men, tense with purpose, whose eyes swivelled to the kitchen hatch every time she poked her head through to take a fat-slicked cargo from Dolores, the waitress. Squashed between the stacks of dishes were meals, uneaten—the beans a terracotta mosaic, the eggs drying out like stranded amphibians.

"Who are these guys?" Dinah said. "Why don't they eat?"

The mystery was cleared when Dolores delivered, along with the next batch of compressed dinners, a collection of crumpled notes. "Dear Dinah—forgive infernal cheek but I qualify as friendless and would like to make your acquaintance with a view to any of the below-mentioned: marriage, sex, ballroom dancing. Yours, etc. . . . "

"Dear Miss, would you believe that, as a married man with a family of ten, I feel entirely alone in this world? My wife does not speak to me, nor any of my children. As you can see, I am well catered for in specific departments, so would be content with telling you my troubles. Yours in fond hope . . . "

"My dear child, I am a priest and have been informed by a colleague that you are good in confession. My box is at your disposal every first Saturday from 3–5 p.m. at the above address. I am low on faith and am very lonely. P.S. I have a preference for Green Spot. Yours in Christ ... "

Pondering the mystery of the green spot she put away her dishes, poured herself a cup of coffee and went out into the café.

She looked around at a roomful of worried men. In another generation they would have dissipated their unhappiness by meeting to talk about revolution or literature or Gaelic sport. Now, the fashion was for happiness and, since no one's parents had it, the instinct for it did not come naturally and they did not know where to look.

"Well, here I am," she said. She lit a cigarette and sat on top of one of the shiny-surfaced tables. "What do you want me to do?"

The men watched her sullenly.

"I am only an immigrant dishwasher," she appealed. "What could I possibly have to offer you?"

"Love!" One fellow shouted out in an aggrieved manner.

The men were mostly in their forties and fifties, in what is known as the prime of life. Some were in suits and some wore labouring clothes. A grey-faced man, whose unsuitably modish sweater showed the tip of a white neck band, must be the poor priest with the preference for green spot. Why did they all look to her and ignore one another when each craved more or less the same thing—companionship? The famed camaraderie of the male sex, which was like the fire of damp wood—all spark and smoke and no warmth—had ceased to be popular. Like vanquished lions that lie back and show their tummies in submission, the men had torn off their ties and exposed the tender skin of the throat. Women neither feared nor admired them and no longer kept order with the services of love.

"Let brotherly love continue," she urged reading from the book she always carried in her handbag. "Be not forgetful to entertain strangers; for thereby some have entertained angels unawares."

CHAPTER 24

Alice was in the attic looking for Christmas decorations. She had a sudden impulse to unearth the silver balls and paper garlands that must have adorned her girlhood Christmases. She couldn't actually recall any visits from Santa, or forest trees laden with ornaments. Certainly they had not featured in the adult festival. A box of crackers on the dinner table and the solemn wearing of paper hats was all that came to mind. Still, the notion persisted that they might be there, glittering under webs like a pharaoh's treasure.

She heard Dinah calling her and beat the dust off her knees and crawled to the trapdoor. There she clung, squealing in shrill dismay. The ladder had been removed and she was marooned, ten feet up in the ceiling.

"Hang on there," Dinah shouted back. "I only borrowed the ladder. I will bring it right away."

"Did you find the decorations?" She appeared with the narrow climbing frame, looking very peculiar but pleased with herself. Her dark hair and the skin of her forehead seemed to have been flecked with custard.

"No, I did not. What were you doing with the ladder? I might have broken bones." Alice manoeuvred herself around and her affronted bottom appeared in the attic doorway.

"Come and see!" Dinah stood on a lower rung and assisted her down.

Alice's head swung back and forth, glum and voiceless, as she eyed the tide of brilliant yellow that had begun to descend her parents' hall wall, engulfing their dignified green.

"Isn't that beautiful? We're going to have some light in this ugly old hall at last."

"Child of grace!" Alice moaned.

"I am glad you think so. As you can see, I have begun to put my plan into action."

It was Dinah's plan to release the house from association with the past by obliterating its hard-wearing colour scheme, which she said consisted of fly-paper beige and cabbage-water green. Alice had been indulgent at the time. Now she found the effect of Dinah's spinach and custard décor deeply upsetting, as if the hairdresser had put a pink stripe in her scalp when she went for a perm.

"Dear child, it will take dozens of coats. The green will keep coming through. What in God's name will it look like?"

"Now that you mention it, it would look like the result of some disturbance in the digestive tract."

"Abominable!"

"You need not worry. That wall will have more coats than Napoleon on his retreat from Moscow. My friends are coming."

"Those friends again! Who are they?"

"Priests, plumbers, politicians." Dinah picked a hairnet of cobwebs from Alice's scalp.

"It's a fable, Dinah. Face up to reality. There are no friends."

"You yourself are famous for this reality, with your wonderful parents and your wonderful childhood and your wonderful amnesia."

"Sarcasm is the wit of fools. My life is an open book."

"Read to me then!" Dinah marched off and returned with her ladder, which she slammed against the wall where the bright yellow beach met the slime-green sea. She climbed up smartly and continued with her jaundicing operation. Alice kept a grim eye on the slithering brush with its devouring intent. It seemed that, as she gazed, a thin rope of light found its way in the fanlight and settled itself upon the shapeless cloud of yellow. She noticed that there was an angel in the corner, moulded in plaster, its features once serenely blanched, now corrupted by a decaying layer of dust.

"I used to pray to that angel once." She pointed shyly to the rotting spirit. "When I was a child. I had forgotten about that. You couldn't really see it in the poor light."

Dinah paused, brush in hand. A glob of yellow made a leisurely parting from the bristles and splattered like an egg yolk upon the carpet's writhing blooms.

"What did you pray for?"

"At first I prayed for a companion—not a child of my own age; I wanted a baby to play with."

Dinah had heard the story of Alice's First Communion and her wasted two and sixpence, many times. She dipped her brush into paint and slapped the wall.

"And later, when I was thirteen, I prayed again."

"For what? A man this time?"

"Well, perhaps, although I hadn't thought of that. I prayed that I would grow thin . . . and adorable."

"Yes?" Dinah pretended to go on with her painting.

"Every year we went on holidays to the sea, the same boarding house in Greystones with a glass panel in a door that was marked 'dining room', through which, at appointed hours, a maid bore tray after tray of glutinous nourishment. It was on that holiday that, for the first and only time, I rebelled against my parents."

The sound of the brush was like the swish of the tide. Dark Dinah, high in her spreading patch of light, looked up at the angel's smug beneficence and thought it fair enough that she had been condemned to earthly corruption and the humiliations of geriatric housekeeping. All the same she might find a lick of white for her face. Alice, down below in the green, stared at her feet in anger.

"The children I had watched every year on the beach were all growing into adults, with nice hair and pretty figures. I

138

was a shapeless lump. I told Mother I could no longer eat starchy food. She did not seem to understand, for she instructed the waitress to add yet more mashed potato or custard or jam pudding to my plate. Mother tried to make me see sense. 'If you do not eat what is put before you, you will get consumption and die. You will waste away!'"

She wrapped her arms tightly around her body and sank into a crouch. Perhaps it was just for comfort's sake, but she looked like a madwoman in a straitjacket.

"And I did! After two weeks of resistance and a week before my fourteenth birthday, I began to bleed. I was back at school and I discovered it in a lavatory between classes. There was no one I could speak to. A nun had given me a holy picture with a curative formula for cripples on the back. It exhorted a five-day vigil with an hour a day spent before a shrine on five consecutive days. I knelt and prayed. On the sixth day, I was cured. As a warning, I was visited by the illness every month and each month I prayed and was healed. As a penance I ate all that was put before me. It was a year before I learnt that this ... thing ... happens to all women with or without milk puddings."

"Happy times," Dinah whispered.

Alice hauled herself up on hearing Dinah. "Ho, yes! We weren't teenagers in those days, nor adolescents. We were boys and girls. It meant that you did what you were told and you didn't have money to burn."

Later on, when they were having their tea, she surprised Dinah. "I did once, you know, pray for a man."

Dinah carefully spooned pickle onto her toasted cheese and ham.

"I was in my thirties. I thought the game was up. I did a novena in Whitefriars Street church." She chortled bashfully and cut herself a slice of cream sponge, freshly thawed. "I don't suppose I was ever all that interested in men—as *such*— but I wanted, you know, some sort of life of my own."

"What about your prayers? Were they answered?"

Alice made a face. "If you like. Poor Gosling! My parents soon made me see he only wanted a roof over his head."

"It's not an unreasonable desire," Dinah suggested. "Tell us about this Gosling."

"We met in Roberts Café. I was having lunch and he sat down and told me his name. Burton Gosling. I remember feeling sorry for him because there were white flecks around his mouth, from those powders you take for indigestion. When I got up to leave he said he'd like to see me again—to take me out. 'You name it!' he said—'tea in the Capital, the pictures, cocktails in the Palace Bar!' I suppose the novena had made me reckless. I said yes. We went out to the pictures, oh, a dozen times and he always bought a half-pound of sweets for us to eat. Once he kissed me on the hair."

"Did you like that?"

"I don't know. I couldn't breathe. He told me ... he loved me."

"What did you say?"

"Well, I laughed. What else? Such foolishness. He had a clever line of talk. I do remember that. He even managed to say nice things about my looks. He seemed keen enough—all talk, as I later found out."

"What did this devil do to you?"

"He came to tea."

"Pretty bad!"

"I thought it would be nice to ask him home to meet my parents—not that I had any intention of ... " She bustled nervously and plucked at her slice of sponge. "I remember being disappointed about the tea. Mother wouldn't let me go to any trouble. She said it didn't do to show one's hand, so there was only the old Delft and a teapot with a crack, which I'd never even seen before—and doorstep sandwiches of cheese and onion. Burton brought a Fuller's cake.

"The garden was lovely though." She laughed. "The four

of us sitting together in the evening sun, chatting like old friends! But then he said he wanted to see my father alone. Well, Father scuttled off. He was no use at that sort of thing. Mother always took over. 'You can talk to me, young man,' she smiled. 'Not young, actually. You're no spring chicken!' She said that to him. She told me to go inside and see to the tea.

"I listened. I listened through the scullery window. He told mother he was ... devoted to me. 'So are we!' mother said. She had taken his arm. She appeared to be leading him around the lawn on a forced march. 'We have devoted all our lives to her. She has never had to do a hand's turn. What have you got to offer her? Capital? motor car? property? club membership?' He failed. He failed me. Even then he did not go away but told her he wanted to marry me. Mother looked at him in silence. She was furious. She was speechless with fury. She leaned over as if to confide in him and ... was ill ... over his boots."

"I hope he offered her a stomach powder," Dinah said.

"He kept walking after her. She walked away but he followed her. He looked ridiculous with his soiled boots."

"You could have gone to him." Dinah sounded fed up. "You could have given him a cloth to clean his boots."

"Mother came back into the house. He tried to follow but she had closed the door. 'He is simply looking for somewhere to hang up his hat.' That is what she told me. Burton was outside the window. He was trying to wipe his boots with a bunch of leaves.

"'There are plenty of rooms here,' I tried to reason with mother. 'Don't be a fool, girl,' Mama said. Poor Mama! I was such a fool. 'Don't you know the first thing about men?'

"She told me. She told me horrible things that would happen to me night after night, and my parents, under the same roof, would be unable to answer my cries because he would be married to me and it would be his right to use me as he wished. Of course I knew about the married act, but I had no idea, until poor Mother told me, that it would be so painful, so brutal.

"I was very shocked by what she said. I was profoundly disappointed in Mr. Gosling, but even then, I could not let the matter lie. 'If I was married,' I told poor Mama, 'I would do my duty the same as any other woman.'"

"'You would have to take off all your clothes,' she said, 'and get into bed with a naked man!'"

"'No!' I tried to stop her, for I knew she hated having to mention such things. 'There is nightwear available—of course there is—with apertures for that business.'

"Mother laughed at me. In spite of her own upset, she laughed. I could see Burton staring at me in the window, so intent, and in that moment I imagined that he was picturing me without my clothes. 'Go away!' I shouted."

"In that case, I suppose he went." Dinah filled Alice's teacup, as solemnly as if it was a sanctuary lamp.

"We never saw him again." Alice reached for her tea and surveyed the wreckage of her plate of sponge. "Mother was right after all. No gumption!"

"So you never got to see a naked man?" Dinah said.

"Indeed I did!" Alice was dismissive.

"You are full of surprises," Dinah smiled.

"*Life* is full of surprises."

So it was that intimacy invaded her life, not with the fabled braggadoccio of sanctified virile lust, but in the ancient intimate dependencies of her own, good, fastidious parents— not just night after night, but day after day and night after night. Not, after all, so terrible or shocking; menial, helpless, unimportant, sour.

Alice considered the cream sponge and decided it would be wasteful to cut herself a fresh slice. All the same, she did.

CHAPTER 25

Dinah's friends came. It filled Alice with dismay. Rough, hairy fellows stood jesting in the hall with the black woman and then meekly accepted paintbrush or hammer and went to work under her direction.

She really had friends! Alice's childhood had been saturated in poems and essays on the subject of friendship. It existed in her imagination as had the foreign woman's notion of snow, impossibly pure and deep. Impossible.

"This house is like a railway station," she complained to Dinah. She gave her high, warning laugh. "I hardly know what to do with myself. I feel it is I who am the intruder."

"There are no intruders," Dinah said firmly. "There are guests and you are the hostess."

"I don't know what to do."

"Hospitality, I believe, is the keynote. Can you bake a cake?"

"I once made a Victoria sandwich." Alice shook her head gravely. "It fell."

"Did not Jesus forgive the fallen woman?" Dinah confusingly reproved.

When Alice went into the kitchen she found a man angrily trying to tear up the lino. He wore dull grey and his scalp showed florid through mongrel strings of hair. Unlikely instinct told Alice that no one loved such a creature, that his wife curtailed her conversation when he entered the room and responded to his touch as to rain under the collar.

He saw her then and stood up, crossly wielding some nail-pulling implement. His face had the stricken look of a leaf when it is first touched by frost. What she saw was that the grey jacket was part of a suit. Here was a man in a suit and she was making a fool of herself. She scuttled out backwards, apologising. "Forgive me. I was going to make a cake."

At once the menace fell away from him. "A cake? Come back out of that and don't mind me. Would there be a cup of tea on the go?"

She edged back into the room. "I'll put the kettle on. I'm Miss Boyle. I'm Alice."

"Marcus Murgatroyd!" The hand that he offered her seemed like a knuckle of ham, so little did it compromise to her grip. She recognised now that its rigour stemmed from fear, the same fear that made her own hand shrink, boneless, inside another person's grasp. With an effort she said, "You are kind to have come. You have put yourself out for us."

He watched her in perplexity, as if she had posed a difficult question, but then his face lit up. "A nice Child-of-Mary blue, I thought!" He indicated her seeping walls. "After we've dealt with the matter of the floor which, if you'll pardon my saying, is a death trap."

"A hell hole!" Alice said with feeling, and she laughed. "Well, here's me wasting time and you wanting your tea."

"He hummed while he tore at fragments of rotting floorboard. His mood had changed since Alice came to keep him company.

She experienced a sense of great achievement as if she had tamed some wild and unusual beast.

Unearthing her baking utensils she was reminded of an earlier time when she had sought to attract Mrs. Willoughby's attention by flailing father's spade. Everything was covered with rust and tiny insects fled before her giant eye. With a Brillo she got the barnacles off and then she set about rooting out some recipe books. Most of them seemed to date back to the war and were devoted to the uninteresting task of cooking without anything. At last she found a prescription for Victoria sponge, which at least she had practised once before, and she cracked the eggs into fat and flour and sloshed them about with a fork.

After the amalgamated mess had gone into the oven, the smell was glorious. It drew men from all parts of the house. When they put their heads around the scullery door Alice coyly waved a teapot and knew the feeling of power.

The cake emerged from the oven with the appearance of a creature trapped in a fire. Dark and flat, its porous surface made it look like something recently deprived of hair, and perhaps legs. Molten carbon from the oven ceiling had rained black spots on its surface. She clutched it with a teacloth, out of view of the men, and gave it a poke. The texture was revolting, at once hard and yielding. With a little mew of distress she thrust it into a cupboard and was about to shut it in there when she saw, at the back, an old bag of icing sugar and some forgotten jam. She sprinkled a good handful of the lumpy icing on top of the scorched confection and coaxed the cloudy jam into its gooey centre.

The table was set with a rusting lace cloth and the best china. The cake sat on top of a tiered stand with a few Mr. Kipling's on the bottom deck.

Hardened men snivelled when they saw this display. The cake, sectioned into dainty slices and consumed with pints of tea, received no detailed critical review. "Oh, that's class, that's idyllic," one guest burped with satisfaction, retrieving with his tongue a trail of uncooked cake mixture.

"Our wives and mothers do not cook any more," another fellow complained. "It's all microwave and boil in the bag. They buy cakes from the shops."

Contentment broke out in the ranks so that they were compelled to sing. Alice was fêted with patriotic ballads, hymns and American country and western. When the tea was finished, Dinah topped the dregs with whiskey.

145

"I think they like my cake," Alice confided, her cheeks puce with attention.

Dinah put an arm around her. "I am sure they never tasted anything like it."

The men left after tea.

"Come again," Alice urged them.

"Of course they will come," Dinah said. "There is still work to be done in the house. When it is finished we'll have a housewarming party and everyone can bring their wives."

"They don't want us," Marcus Murgatroyd lamented. "They have the children."

Dinah said, "The children belong to no one but themselves. Women fill their arms with them because there is no one else. Just because you don't answer their needs and they don't answer your demands doesn't mean they aren't lonely too."

"What do you know about it?" said an animated gnome who described himself as O'Herlihy. "You try talking to my woman. Maria Goretti O'Herlihy won't let me sit down at the dinner table. She says I burnt my boats with other women years ago."

Dinah smiled. It was heartening to think that there were women who would assist a gnome in the toasting of his fleet. "Bring your wife a little present. Do not hand it to her for years of resentment will bring an unkind response to her mouth but put it somewhere she will find it, with a note to say that you miss her. I think you will find your boats can still be re-launched."

When he was leaving, O'Herlihy said to Alice. "She's a lovely woman, your daughter."

Alice looked in alarm across the room to where the plump, baby-featured foreigner was deep in mirth with a gathering of her disciples. "She is a good-natured thing," she smiled.

"Now that, if you'll forgive me, is a masterpiece of under-statement. Myself, I think she is some class of a prophet."

Alice laughed uneasily. She liked holy scripture in its place

146

but to think of it rising off the pages was unsettling. On her way to the hall door she noticed that the application of yellow paint had been completed. The venerable slime green had been vanquished. The clocks no longer lurked in shadows. Out of the ceiling a radiant angel smiled.

CHAPTER 26

Sometimes Dinah still got a pain in her heart. Alone in the night she banged at the door of heaven like the man who knocked upon his neighbour's dwelling demanding bread but she knew there was a flaw in the theory of receipt on demand. Like the feckless host, she had left it too late, she had failed to employ her opportunities and resources. She ached for home, not knowing where that was. She would settle, though, for someone to scratch her back.

She had done well. The café where she worked was now a celebrated spot. Hundreds thronged to hear her words or, in effect, the word of the Lord. There were negotiations for the lease of the next-door premises, an all-purpose store with sidelines in tailoring alterations, denture repairs and the rental of video films.

She no longer washed the dishes. She had been made manageress. She was given a free hand and had authorised a number of changes. There was good bread on the wooden tables which replaced the old red plastic laminate. The deathly, quaking, purplish bars of fluorescent had been prised from the ceiling and shaded lamps installed at low level, with their wiring concealed. Mindful of the happy miracle at Cana, she had made application for a wine licence.

It was a pleasant place with simple food. Everyone liked fish and chips. Although it had not been a specific part of her plan, it was beginning to make a large profit and Dinah, her wage substantially bolstered, had been offered a share in profits in case she took it into her head to leave.

The unkempt and heartsick were now joined by a more

148

stylish clientèle, young professionals and married couples, eager for some new experience which would not lead to addiction or contagion. At eleven o'clock, when the café was at its fullest, Dinah said grace. Afterwards she walked among the tables, sitting down to speak with those who had troubles on their minds. Around midnight she read a little bit of scripture. There was a homeless boy, who came in to spend the earliest hours of the morning there in warmth and ate a free supper, in return for which he played poignantly on the flute to accompany Dinah's reading. His name was O Dualaing, a Gaelic name which translated beautifully as Son of the Dark Lake.

Now that it was fashionable, the estranged wives of Dinah's earliest customers began to accompany the husbands they had reviled. In this way, some relationships were repaired, at least on the outside, although one or two of the women, released from the solitary confinement of home, had struck up warm relationships with other wives and plotted to abscond to Greenham Common.

She had come a long way since she arrived with nothing but a single address. There were those who would be mightily impressed. She herself could not exult. In reality she was no more than an entertainment, a star attraction. She saw herself as a one-eyed king in the land of the blind. She had no special skills except those of housework and directness. She was not enlightened, except in the sense that light was in her blood. She was a novelty for childish people in a dank playground where snow fell as mud, where the sun was not strong enough to ripen a banana.

December came and with it a sudden warm spell with clattering showers of rain and a weak sun that wobbled like aspic. She went along to St. Stephen's Green, because it reminded her of Figgis, who called it the ducks' palace, and because it was where lovers went and she liked to look at their faces, tender and transformed. She chose a bench whose gaps were darned with the soft skeletons of leaves, and sat by the pond to watch the ducks.

There was a wedding party grouped at the other side of the water, posing for a photograph. "Smile," the photographer urged. "You're none of yis smiling."

"Black teeth!" said the mother of the bride, and everyone laughed. The ducks pedalled and honked in apprehension. "They're not the only thing," said a burly bridesmaid and the party splayed with gaiety and demonstrated teeth which were indeed not in peak condition.

In the middle stood the groom, a small man, his clothing expensive and discreet, his skin as black as ebony. He looked stunned at his good fortune in having married a big white woman with golden hair. It seemed that he had neglected to investigate the family for soon he would be marooned from them by his own manners and breeding. By then, very likely, there would be one or two children of blended colour and he would want to take them home.

After the wedding party had left—pink coats and flowered hats bobbing, the bride's satin dress glinting dully like a shell—there was an odd moment in which the park flexed and then stretched herself. A ripple of pale yellow light spread upon the pond and the grass fanned out silvery depths. The trees sprinkled their last few crumbs of leaf with a toasty sound and the drakes turned sternly to the sky, showing the shot silk of their breasts. Dinah was alone in that moment and she knew that the world had shown her its beauty. It was curious to think that while God neglected her the earth engaged her and gave argument.

In fact it was just that moment before a heavy shower. The clouds turned and swooped and in another second water was pouring down on her like buckets of slop from the sky and she had to put her jacket over her head and make a run for it.

As the miraculous lightening of the park fell more or less

into the category of coincidence, so did the fact that she collided with the belly of her friend, Figgis, who fled from the opposite direction, under cover of a wet *Irish Press*.

Both of them scowled upon impact but neither bothered to show great surprise for each time she sat alone in the park she had at least some hope of seeing him and he now strolled this grassy route from Leeson Street to South King Street daily on the off chance of a glimpse of her brooding black bulk.

For a time they sheltered in a wooden pavilion close to the pond. Women with white parasols might have defended milky complexions against the sun there, when such complexions were the fashion. Now it was used mainly by bands who gave free concerts, or office workers eating picnic lunches, who educated the ducks' appetites with scraps of hamburger or muesli bar. When it became obvious that the shower was persistent, they agreed to make a dash for some more hospitable refuge.

They ran together, not stopping until instinct brought them safely into a steamy lair adjacent to Grafton Street.

"I haven't seen much of you lately." He blew on his hot whiskey and his lips made snarling sorties at its scalding enticement. "Have you been avoiding me?"

"No, dear heart," Dinah said. "I have been busy."

"I know. As a matter of fact I know all about you. You appear to have made quite an impact. Your name is vaunted in respectable public houses. You have become a legend in your own lifetime. You seem to be thought of as some sort of saint. I have heard you referred to as the Black Madonna." She could tell from his voice and the way that he avoided her eye that he was embarrassed saying this. "Are you a saint, Dinah?"

He was hoping to hear her loud, refreshing laugh but she just kept on her bad-tempered and reflective look and threw back her hot drink as if her lips were made of asbestos. "If

151

you are in need of a saint then I am one, for that is the way these things come about. Myself, I prefer the notion of a legend, that being a tale with no verifiable fact. What is it that you want, Figgis?"

"Leather lips, so I can get me drink inside me."

"I was hoping that you wanted nothing. That is how I saw you, Figgis, as a happy ascetic. I wanted to be like you."

"Ah, no, you don't want that. You're a good girl. I'm just a con artist."

"A con artist!" She grinned at him. "That is the perfect description for me. Now give me a kiss and I'll buy you another drink."

When she looked at him she saw that there was something the matter. Without having lost any weight, he had somehow deflated.

"What has happened?" She took his hand, which had the bluntness of a teddy bear's paw.

At first he just shook his head as if words could not frame the calamity.

"Tell me."

"Me wife's come back."

She dropped his hand and sighed. "There. That is all right then. You are loved."

"Get away. She doesn't love me. She can't stand me. I am a toenail in the wash-basin of humanity. She has returned bearing only the gift of her grudges. I am a monetary boil, to be lanced and drained."

"What about the children?" Dinah said.

"They watch me with ferrets' eyes. They steal the loose change from my pocket. They have been told some dire infamy in relation to myself."

Dinah concentrated on a group perched on mahogany stools at the distant end of the bar. Sealed into a bubble of tobacco smoke they appeared to her as a rosy mirage, the rasp of their laughter spicy on the mild spread of placatory

152

talk. So groups of people gathered all over Ireland, she imagined, in public houses or village streets, across garden walls, their faces angelic, their breasts radiant with friendship. "I have a theory," she confided to Figgis. "The people of this country are full of kindness, but always to strangers. When a relationship is required—landlady, mother, husband, wife, complications and hostilities arise. They do not have the facility for intimacy."

"You have the theory, we go one better—we have the formula," Figgis boasted. "Consider, if you will, the supreme discomfort of your average Irish home, the low-wattage bulbs, the poor drainage and heating, the wisps of shattered lino marooned on rotting floorboards. Now witness the high degree of cosseting on offer in a common or garden gargle parlour. We Irish were never intended to live in domesticity. The entire scene is so arranged that we are encouraged to flee the austerity and rebuke of home for the comfort of strangers and the cordiality of the shebeen."

Dinah regarded her surroundings. There was indeed warmth in the dark wooden furnishings, the soft lighting in brass fitments, the banks of yielding seating. Mirrors reflected a shimmering army of glasses, lined·up in their graded sizes like pieces of a chess set, and the liquor bottles showed splinters of jewelled colour where the light engaged their contents.

"Am I right or am I right?" Figgis demanded.

"As always," Dinah quietly agreed.

"No, no. Not always. I only make sense when I'm with you. Why is that, I wonder?"

"Perhaps it is because we are strangers."

"No!"

"No." She regarded him fondly. Each time they met she was less enthusiastic about parting. He was that rare thing, a man of simple comfort and logic. "I suppose," she ventured cautiously, "it might be because I love you."

153

He gave her a murderous look—but she did not mind, she understood that it was only shyness. "Ah, now," he warned. "We haven't had enough drink for that class of talk."

"I am sorry," she said demurely. "Let us have some more." They sat in silence while she made sign language to the stranger behind the bar who without perambulation or rebuke reinforced their ration of cheer. Dinah paid for her round, and Figgis gulped back the boiling drink, puckering his jaws against the pain. In a little while he said in cowering tones: "Ditto, moi."

"I beg your pardon?" she enquired.

"That. What you said. The same goes for me. In regard to yourself, that is."

For a while she frowned at him in confusion and then she gave him one of her giant smiles, which he treasured. "Oh, that. Love! I know that."

As soon as his embarrassment had receded, Figgis began to chortle. "Heh heh! So you like me?"

"At the very least."

He continued to marvel, his reflections punctuated by small grunts of satisfaction, until he was struck by a sense of responsibility. "What are we going to do?"

"Oh, do nothing. That is by far the safest."

"Would you come away with me?"

"What?" It was Dinah's turn to be disconcerted.

"Come live with me and be my love."

"Live where? With your wife and the ferrets?"

"No, Dinah, listen! We'll make the big break, head for your part of the world, bananaland. Where did you say you came from?"

"Brixton."

'Oh, I know, I know. I mean originally."

She shook her head and gave him a smile in which there was some disagreeable element, regret or pity. "I can't come with you."

"Why?"

She said nothing.

He leaned into her silence, reading it. "You were having me on," he declared. "Of course you were. Hah! I'm not much of a prize."

"You are a prize," Dinah said. "I just can't go, not now. I cannot give you any reason. It seems I have some duty to fulfil."

"Sunshine, though! Think of it. We could live on fresh coconuts and fish from the sea. You're a free woman. You're not like me, a lout and a renegade, trampling the hopes of innocent women and children, the drink pouring out of my ears. What would you have in the way of duty?" He answered this himself, beating the side of his head with his hand. "I was forgetting! Your poor little mammy! Of course you can't go gallivanting on a whim. Unless, of course, she'd like to come with us. How is she, by the way?"

Dinah's mood was not to be lightened. Each simple statement and query seemed to cast her deeper into melancholy. She turned to him with such a sad look that he imagined her mother must have been struck down with plague or eaten by wild dogs. "She is not my mother!" Dinah cried.

He backed off. His jaw dropped and his teeth showed in confusion. "Of course she is! Not officially, I know—you explained all that. She bought you from the nuns."

Dinah sighed. "All of that is nonsense. I never heard of her until I arrived in Ireland."

He picked up his glass and brutally eyed its dehydrated floor. He emitted a low growl and then he sighed.

"She herself supplied that story," Dinah said. "I merely agreed to it. In reality I was given her name and address by a salesman of used televisions in return for ten pounds. I met him in a public house soon after I arrived. I asked this man how one could make some money in the city. He informed me that it was a happy hunting ground for thieves due to a

155

large and trusting population of the elderly. He himself did not resort to theft except in case of necessity. Instead he sold faulty television sets to pensioners and then sold their addresses to those even less scrupulous. I would have taken an honest job, Figgis. I had hardly any money. I did not know what else to do."

"What were you going to do to her?" With an air of retribution he set his empty glass in front of her and entitled himself to hers.

"I planned to say that I was from a bible society and gain her trust and access to her house. Failing that I was intending to use a spanner. On her head."

"Why didn't you use the spanner, Dinah? Why didn't you take the money and run?"

There was a silence. Discomfort grew in it like a fungus. "My name is not Dinah," she said at last and in a voice so quiet he could hardly hear. "It was what she called me, employing some recess of her memory when she imagined I had introduced myself. My name is Cora."

"Dinah!" He spoke through teeth unevenly clenched. "Why didn't you?"

"I don't know, Figgis. Something happened. She gave me tea and sherry. She thought an old record player was a coffin. Besides, we had a lot in common. Both of us had spent long years looking after our mothers."

"Ah, there you are! You were subject to the saving grace of your own mother. And didn't you become a daughter to the old wan anyway?"

Dinah shook her head. "I lost touch. She had an accident. I went and visited her in hospital once but we had a row."

Figgis remained hunched into a ragged fugue until Dinah, or Cora, managed to organise further refreshment. When his drink was put before him he thanked her with a rueful smile and allowed his hand to find her knee. "I absolve you in the

156

name of the mother and this mother's son. Sure, you're only a victim of circumstance."

"I'm a fraud, Figgis."

"No, no! Small pockets of dissimulation, no more than that. You're an authentic black from the West of Africa. No one can say otherwise."

"My father was white. I was born in England. I have never been to Africa."

Figgis found this unforgivable. He whipped his hand away and glowered at her. "All that guff about thatched huts on the edge of the jungle! Did you make it up, or what?"

"It's the truth!" She appealed to him, her round face and pouting mouth the picture of innocence so that his heart was sorely tried. "It was my mother's story, which she repeated to me daily, as far back as I can remember. She grew up in Africa. She was brought to England by my white father who abandoned her. After she died, I had nothing left except her stories, so I took them for myself."

She was disturbed by scuffling noises and the unmistakable menace of men's voices roughened with fear or anger. Dissent had broken out within the charmed côterie at the end of the bar. One man was punching another repeatedly on the nose. The victim concentrated on holding his hat on his head. Blood poured from his nose and spilled over his lips.

Figgis had begun to speak, composing his words slowly and thoughtfully. "Dinah—you won't mind if I stick to Dinah, will you ...?" She could not concentrate. Some breath of lawlessness had seeped through the ventilators and was affecting all the harmonious strangers. A man seated in a corner began to fondle the giant breasts of his companion, rubbing them back and forth as if doubtful of their substance. The woman ignored him, circumventing his arm with hers to delicately raise a glass of sherry to her lips. A boy with a face like Jesus began a lank but intrusive recital on a Spanish guitar.

157

"Figgis, what is happening?" Dinah looked bewildered.

He glanced around impatiently. "Nothing! Listen to me, Dinah. My offer still stands."

"I'm listening. Look! A young woman in combat clothing is pouring a pint of beer over the barman."

"Take no notice. It's the hour that's in it. When the drink reaches a certain level in the brain, sincerity asserts itself and all hell breaks loose. It is a nightly occurrence about this time."

"What time is it?"

"It's ten o'clock."

"I'm late for work. I've got to go."

"Yes or no, Dinah?"

She stood up to go and then bent again to kiss him on the forehead. "Would to God ye would bear with me a little in my folly," she said softly.

"Amn't I after accepting you lock, stock and barrel?" He said in an anguish of aggravation.

"No. You are making excuses for me."

Figgis watched her walk away. She no longer wore an anorak but some substantial ethnic garment of red wool lined with sheepskin. She was wearing new boots. She had even made up a new name for herself. Cora!

He found that he did not believe a word of her story about the spanner and the white father. There wasn't a drop of bleach in her. She was black Dinah, who had been bought for two and sixpence. Why would she improvise so queer a yarn? It could only be that what they were saying around town was true, she was some class of a saint, and humility compelled her to heap ashes of infamy on her own head.

He shuddered with unease and suffered a sudden unexpected hankering for his own wife, Peggy, whose pale, suspicious eye had supervised his successful procreative endeavours, whose history was as plain as her hostility.

He ordered another hot port but the bloodstained beverage

seemed abominable in the absence of romantic company. So he sang a song.

The hour of sincerity having passed, the barman had to come over and tell him to contain himself.

CHAPTER 27

Something was happening in the garden. Strange little patches of colour, petals soft as cloth, were clawing their way out of the earth. Nuggets of mud lodged in their folds, giving them the look of something born blind and unable to preen or else something discharged untimely from the earth, like Lazarus.

The small winter plants grew close to the ground in ready-made bouquets; whorls of purple or a scattering of gold, like spilled spices; a plant the pink of a felt hat; largish daisies with gauzy petals veined with mauve and a fuzzy plum-coloured button in their centre.

Alice had taken to a morning perambulation in the early hours while Dinah still slept. She wanted to catch the garden out in the act of transformation, but always it had been up and at work before her. This morning, a tangle of dead twigs, thin and bare as string, had borne down on some unseen nurturing station and released tiny flourishes of brilliant yellow like magician's hankies.

It was a phenomenon. Flowers did not bloom in the depths of December. Maybe they did. Maybe the foolish ones were lured out by the unseasonal spell of mild weather. Surely there would have to be something there already in the earth to lure. It was only a month since Dinah had begun her reclamation of the garden, since she had pushed in the tiny onions with their graveyard markers, the seeds as unprom-ising as mouse droppings.

One day, passing a dull scribble of shrub, she was overcome by a perfume so intense that it seemed to exude heat. She turned quickly, imagining she would catch it out in some deceit, but the perfume remained and when she looked closely she saw that the dull leaves shielded clusters of tiny buds, creamy white with a lick of pink. She touched one and it shivered.

Odd occurrences no longer unnerved her. Dinah had made her see that we live with ghosts and miracles; that in the natural world nothing is strange before God and nothing quite known to man. She was learning every day. In the garden one does not grow old. The birds and cats did not call her old. If she wanted, she could lie down under this unkempt, whorish, unsuitably ornamented growth and it would not think her foolish. Strapped up in religion all her life, she had never believed in God. Dinah believed. "How do you *know*?" Alice pursued. "Who else would let a fly fly?" Dinah demanded.

As often happened when she was thinking of Dinah, the black woman appeared, apparently from nowhere. Wrapped in her dressing gown, she held out a cup of steaming tea to Alice. "Korean Viburnum," she boomed at her sternly.

"Lyons Green Label was alway good enough for us," Alice observed mildly.

"Not the tea—the tree!" Dinah laughed. "I saw you admiring it. Another of God's jokes. If only we could take a leaf from nature's book, we would learn to balance our own. Plain women should wear immoral perfume. It makes people look twice."

"That's all very well," Alice said; "but where's its calendar? It's December and the garden's a riot of colour."

"Not so much a riot as a small gesture of defiance. You would have made a good news reporter, the way you exaggerate. The weather is mild and the garden, being walled, is exceptionally sheltered."

"Have you seen what's going on?"

"Winter aconite, winter jasmine, Christmas rose ... "

"Where did they come from?"

"Ah, now! There's a question."

"You planted them not a month ago. I saw you buying seeds and putting them down."

"Not me! Not these ones."

"I don't understand."

"They were there all along, buried under briars, deep asleep like the Sleeping Beauty. They were planted by your father, years and years ago. They are winter flowers, meant to relieve the gloom of winter. Buried in undergrowth, they were unable to bloom—or perhaps they did and you could not see. Do you know that story, by the way, the Sleeping Beauty? Woken by a kiss! A ridiculous fable. After all those years asleep her mouth would have tasted like a lumberman's laundry bag."

Father's garden, stumbling over the seasons to come back to her. She could not quite believe that such tiny, delicate plants were meant to expose themselves to winter cold, could have found the courage to come out after the black chill of November.

"A winter garden is a child's garden," Dinah said. "All the flowers lie close to the ground. Some of them you have to be quite small even to see. In summer the garden is an explosion of colour, not entirely tasteful. That is for the adult eye, short of sight and darkened by depression."

"Oh, you're wrong," Alice said. She bent to examine some miniature gold sunrays, pressed close against their leathery leaves, like earrings. "I had a very dim eye as a child. I used to feel like Alice in Wonderland, too large for everything around me, one foot in the chimney and the other in my mouth." She patted the little flower and beamed ruefully at Dinah. "It wasn't until I grew up that I fitted my size. I wasn't a beauty but I was the same as any young girl. All young girls are lit up, aren't they? And I was in love."

"Yes, you told me. Mr. Gosling—the one with the stomach

powders. Your mother got sick on his boots."

"Oh, no, that was nothing. That was much later. This was the real thing." She stood up, beating at her lower half, to release brittle limbs.

That evening Dinah brought her into the city for a look at the Christmas lights and a drink in Wynn's Hotel. Wynn's was Alice's choice. It was where priests went and so it was respectable. They talked of this and that, of Christmas shopping and the care of plants, until several cocktails had been consumed and then Alice took Dinah's hands in her own and rubbed them imploringly with her fingers. "He wasn't *suitable*!"

"You don't have to tell me," Dinah said.

"Oh, but I do—you'll see," Alice muttered.

"All right, my child," Dinah smiled. "It seems as good a place as any for confession, since we are surrounded by God's holy ministers. What made your lover unsuitable? Did he speak with the accent of the city?"

"His accent was all right. He was a doctor."

"Quite a catch! Married then?"

"I would never have gone out with a married man!"

"Of course not." Dinah inhaled deeply for patience. "Wrong God?"

Alice shrugged and looked away. "Perhaps, but anyway the same as mine."

"So what was the terrible disgrace of this doctor? Was his name, by any chance, Crippen?"

"His name was Makwaia. Dr. Henry Makwaia."

"Aah." Dinah withdrew herself and gave attention to her drink.

"He was ... coloured. In those days we said 'coloured'. It was, in fact, a more accurate word than black. He wasn't black, more a sort of greyish brown, a very gentle colour. He was older than me. His hair was grey too. He wasn't a handsome man but he was a beautiful colour."

163

"Why didn't you tell me this before?" Dinah's voice was still pleasant enough but her cheeks showed a sullen bulge.

"I told no one. I never intended to tell anyone. We saw each other in secret for two years. As far as my parents were concerned, I was going out with Bea Madigan. I couldn't have brought a black man home to mother. That would have been the end."

"Perhaps you were relieved, in one way, to have to keep it a secret."

"It shocked me to be seen out with a coloured man, yes." Even now Alice lowered her voice and looked around, forgetting, since no one was looking at her, that her companion failed to conform. "In another way I was glad, because he was clever and sophisticated and I thought he wouldn't have bothered with me if he was a white man. When there was nobody else to look I didn't notice his colour."

"It sounds like a reasonable arrangement. I'm surprised you aren't still sneaking off to meet Bea Madigan."

"Ho, no! It was a fool's paradise. The game was soon up. Someone saw us together and told my mother. There was a bit of a song and dance. Mother referred to him as the Minstrel Boy." Alice gave a whimper of mirth and then sighed and fell silent. "Of course I denied it all. I even laughed at poor Mother's awful jokes. I said he was a foreigner who had lost his way and I was giving him directions."

She waited for Dinah to criticise her. Hemmed in by priests and sunk in the lounge's sombre plush, her dark daughter seemed more a goddess than a Godless savage, and Alice meekly awaited judgement.

"It's time we were going," was all she said. "We'd better go to the toilet first." She stood to help Alice to her feet.

"It was only after I lost him that I realised how much I loved him," Alice appealed, refusing to respond to Dinah's pull. "You see, we got on too well together. There weren't the highs and lows that force other couples to evaluate their affections. We just … got on. I never knew until afterwards that that was intense happiness. I'm a fool, Dinah." She scurried to keep pace with the other's departing stride. "I've known it ever since. Of course, as soon as you accept the shape of your figure, you dress accordingly. I became an animal-lover. I emptied my heart at the paws of cats. As for them, they observed my weakness and exaggerated their plight."

Outside the powder room Dinah paused, as if listening for something. "It's over now," she said. "Perhaps it was all for the best."

"No! You can't think that!"

"I wasn't thinking of you. I was thinking of your doctor. Times don't really change, you know. Only patterns of education and economic necessity."

She tried to picture herself as a young Mrs. Makwaia, wheeling a pram, braving the stares. "Yes," Alice said.

At the time she had grieved so deeply that her whole body went into rebellion and the blood that she feared so much when she was fourteen dried up and never came again. She could not go against her parents. When the misery had exhausted itself, life went on as before. She was left, at the age of twenty-five, placidly in middle age.

Now she stood at the washroom mirror watching herself, not in the way that women do to come to terms with their faces, but with the wary curiosity of strangers.

"My mother," she reflected quietly, "was a bit of a termagant."

She berated her nose indifferently with an old grey powder puff, like the rouged corpse of a mouse.

"My father wasn't a saint either. I can see that now—and something else. I take after him. I always knew I hankered after a bit of cheer but it's more than that. I'm attracted by vulgarity. Mother used to say he was a vulgar little man. She

. anted me to despise him too, but the nearest I could get was to deny his nature: my nature."

"Why are you saying all this now?" Dinah smeared pearl shadow on her lids. She was getting ready for work.

"It's because of you, dear. You are all honesty. You are a blessing. You have taught me not to fear the truth."

Small and badly worn, she stood before her giant child. Never in her life had she blurted out her feelings in such a manner. She hoped that Dinah would touch her—a hug or a pat. She realised that she had come to love her, not with the swift and violent adulation she had felt for Mrs. Willoughby, but in the slow enchanting manner that hidden virtue brings and easy acceptance and the prolonged absence of boredom. They got on.

"I hear music," Dinah said. "Sounds like a band. Let's go have a look."

They crept along the carpeted corridor, arm in arm, until they came to the pulsating chamber which was marked, "Function. Private." For a whole tune they stood outside, Alice with tapping toes, Dinah with acoustic hips. An interval came with gentle clapping and a fuzz of talk. Alice opened the door a crack. "It's some sort of an office do," she reported back. "There's a combo."

The door was eased back by inches until Alice was inside. She grinned back in triumph at Dinah. "They won't mind us. We'll just watch one dance and then we'll go."

Brushing the drums, tickling the piano and fondling the bass, the musicians prepared for the singer's passionate, bellowing version of "My Way". With raised eyebrows and a smile Alice signalled to Dinah that they were in luck. Dinah was laughing and Alice laughed back, although she couldn't think why, for she could not see the moustached, middle-aged lothario bearing down on her.

"Arbroath Smokie!" said the man—or something like that, for he had an accent of assumed grandeur which made him hard to understand. He touched her shoulder and then swept her off in a sort of tango. She submitted to this with no protest, her wool coat flailing and her mohair beret clinging to wisps of her hair.

Dinah waited for the set to end before she went to claim her parent. She did not want to spoil her fun, but she had to get to work and she wanted to see Alice safely on the bus.

"You go on, dear," Alice urged. "Ambrose is leaving me home." She managed a look of indifference but her cheeks burned fiercely and she looked younger somehow, fluffier.

Her feet, in their little zipped boots, moved off at a blissful gallop as her partner thrust her through a sea of resentfully rustling taffetas and Tricels.

CHAPTER 28

"I have decided," Alice announced, "to give some dibs to the girls. To Marjorie and Andrea."

"So long as they have poisoned tips on them" It was Christmas Eve and Dinah was doing the decoration. Tall candles, nesting in holly, brought splendour to the gilt frame of father's mottled overmantel. There was a Christmas tree, burdened with balls and fragile lights that dimmed and glowed with nervous frequency.

"Dibs, dear!" Alice swayed regally around the room, a glass in hand, approving the effects. "A few bob to tide them over until they can benefit from my popping off."

She felt a bit guilty. The children's visit would not be the highlight of former years. Dinah was having a party. She had encouraged Alice to ask friends of her own. Alice said she didn't know anyone. The children would only accuse her of burning money. "What about that man from Wynn's— Arbroath Smokie?" Dinah persisted. The older woman laughed it off. "He had a short pocket and a long cough." The truth was, the evening had become a blur. All she could remember clearly was the glorious interlude of the tango. She could not even recall her partner's proper name.

Although the feast was still twelve hours off, she had laid the table in readiness so that she could admire it. Out had come the good tablecloth, its rust covered by pieces of china. The spoons were polished and instead of ordinary sugar there were pink crystals like bath salts. A pyramid of bought mince pies vied with Alice's cake, a labour of unseasoned love with icing flung over it like a wet towel. There was a trifle with a

Santa sinking sideways into the custard. A profusion of edible favours had bled, with a poignant echo of King Arthur's Table, man by man fallen in Lyonesse about their lord. Cheese straws and crisps were going stale in a variety of containers, and twinkling glasses, established beside the teacups, forestalled any possible disappointment.

Oh, it was lovely, lovely. Alice glugged Asti Spumante and trilled a snatch of "Silent Night". She went to have a look at their home-made crib on the sideboard, nicely guarded by a hedge of bottles. "Happy Birthday!" She raised her glass to the rose-tinged youth who lounged so insouciant beneath the solemn gaze of the cow and the carpenter. "What a birthday we're going to have, boy. Thank you for being born, dear Jesus. Thank you for giving us Christmas!"

When she had finished her prayer she found that Dinah was no longer at the mantelpiece, fiddling with the holly. She was standing in the doorway, clad for the street in coat and hat.

"Where are we going?" Alice said at once. "Are we going to midnight mass?"

"You are going to bed." Dinah said firmly. "I am going to work."

"But it's Christmas Eve! Don't you ever get a night off?"

"Not tonight. It's the loneliest night of the year for those with no one to care for them."

Alice was peeved by this interruption to her idyll. She was the one who should be cared for. "All those years I had no one I did not go gallivanting in the small hours of Christmas morning."

"Well, that's a pity. It would have done you good." Dinah came and kissed her on her freshly corrugated hair. "You need an early night tonight. It's a big day tomorrow. I've put a hot water bottle in your bed."

Alice gave a small, self-centred sigh of alcoholic grief.

"Tell you what! I'll bring home chips," Dinah promised.

"Then you will be every bit as fortunate as my over-indulged unloved."

"Off you go!" Alice affected slight but she was thawed by the prospect of a midnight feast.

Whenever Dinah deserted her she had to contend with the fear that she might not see her again. Desolation pawed at her sleeve but she was able to shake it off, for Dinah was everywhere now—in her head, in the beams of her house, in the glowing colours of her walls and even in the flames that cavorted in grates once chill with unuse.

Such an excavation the re-opening of the drawing-room grate had been! Dead magpies rained down the chimney and soot bulged out in its feathery blackness. Everything had been destroyed except solid wood and glass. There was nothing for it but to redecorate and now the room was a nest of pinks and reds.

What would the children say when they saw the mahogany heirlooms warping and groaning in the furnace-blast of Dinah's Christmas fire? Alice pushed another log among the coals. Sometimes she wondered about the cost. The cash that was fed into new comforts and renovations, into nightcaps and Rossiners and pick-me-ups must surely be beyond her resources. Dinah paid her share. She was more than generous. One wondered about that too. The wages of a dish-washer in Alice's day would not have covered the cost of the new colour television set which had been Dinah's Christmas present to Alice.

She would not spoil it with her morbid doubts. One more little drink while she listened to one of Father's records and then she would take herself off to bed.

"O-o-oh, for the wings, for the wings of a d-o-o-ve ... " She sang along with Father, neither of them having much luck with the high notes. Dear old fellow. She never tired of hearing him now. It astonished her that she had once been afraid of his ghost. Ghosts were only old friends, worn out to a shadow.

When his song was ended, Father did not immediately go away. There was the usual gritty silence and then she thought she heard him sigh.

"Oh, that I had wings like a dove. For then would I fly away and be at rest. Lo, then would I wander far off, and remain in the wilderness. Selah."

"Selah!" Alice returned companionably. She put the record back in its sleeve and caught sight of one of the clocks. It was almost midnight. Where had the time gone? She was always saying that lately.

She went to bed. As she succumbed to pleasant thoughtlessness, she remembered that the clocks had not been wound. "Selah!" she insubordinately tooted and turned over to sleep.

Only minutes after that the knock came. Alice woke immediately for she had left some part of herself on vigil for Dinah's return with the chips. "Why doesn't she use her key?" she thought as she fumbled for her cardie. She had the front door open by the time it dawned on her that of course Dinah would have used her key, or if she had lost it would have shouted through the letter-box to declare herself.

"Burglars!" Alice hurled her body at the door, banging it shut in the nick of time. She stood with her back to it, shuddering terribly, her legs softening as she slowly sank into a crouch.

"Let me in," cried the creature.

Alice stopped shaking. She pulled herself to her feet and opened the door. If anyone had asked her afterwards she would have found it difficult to say why. She knew why, but she would have found it difficult to say.

It was the voice. It was exactly like the miaow of a cat.

A girl stood out in the black drizzle: Paper-thin, pale as lard, her painted mouth a stain of Smarties on her deathly skin. She looked familiar but perhaps Alice was just thinking of a film she had once seen, *The Bride of Frankenstein.*

"What do you want?" she managed to say.

"I want to come in."

"Oh, dear no, I don't think so. It's after midnight."

"I've nowhere. You said if ever I needed help. You gave me a fiver." The girl was trembling as Alice had recently been. She had a canvas hold-all and she clutched it tightly to her chest as if it was a doll or a teddy.

"Who are you?" Alice said. The girl's thin hair stood up exactly like the fur of a neglected animal. Well, she could give her a glass of warm milk on the doorstep. One would do as much for an animal.

"I'm Verity!" The girl miaowed.

"Verity?" Alice pulled at her lower lip. She pulled the door open a little more to let the light out and noticed the girl's high heels, her cheap black coat which showed a short skirt underneath. "The fallen woman!" She exclaimed with pleasure, although she could have bitten her tongue off.

At once she ushered her in. It was the delightful young woman who had delayed her in an alleyway to tell her the interesting story of the winter storage of men's private parts. Dinah would be pleased that she had captured such an exotic. And for once she had not shied away from *life.*

The girl stepped into the hall. Alice tried to relieve her of her coat and bag. "Leave them alone!" Her voice was shrill as she defended her possessions. "Just tell me where to put them."

"Dear child!" Alice said. Where to put them? Of course a bed would have to be found. There was the maid's room, but she quickly rejected that notion, remembering the unreasonable way in which Dinah had reacted.

"You're going to put me out after all, aren't you?" Verity jiggled her hold-all in anxiety.

"No, I'm thinking." The bed that Dinah occupied was a good double, had housed her parents and their differences

172

for more than half a century. Dinah would scarcely notice the poor waif in the bed beside her and Verity looked too done in to care.

"I'll have to put you in with someone else for tonight," she said.

Verity's eyebrows shot up. Beneath her tufty hair one imagined that her ears flattened.

"Only another lady!" Alice soothed.

She growled acceptance and Alice led her to her parents' room.

She switched on the light and pulled back a patch of bed. "I'm sure you'll be very comfortable. There's plenty of room," she encouraged. "Would you like anything? A glass of milk?"

"Milk—oh, Christ, yes," Verity said and Alice departed with cowardly relief. The girl was changed. She had grown graceless and bad-tempered. Perhaps she had had some terrible shock. She didn't look too sprightly.

As she carried the steaming glass up the stairs she rehearsed a fresh onslaught of charity. "Is there anything on your mind, dear?" "Would you like to talk?" But, when she got to the room, there was nothing to talk to but a hand, which emerged through a narrow opening of the door, took her supper and slammed it shut again.

"Well!" Alice hoped Dinah would hurry home and show her the way to breathe warmth into society's rejects. She could do with someone to breathe warmth into her feet too. She climbed back into bed, wishing she could undo the episode or wake up to Dinah's cheerful bustle and discover that it had all been a dream. The thought occurred then; perhaps it was a dream. It had the unpleasant, unmalleable qualities of a nightmare. She pinched herself but she was too numb with cold to feel anything. "I don't know where I am," she thought in sudden panic. "Oh, Dinah! Oh, Papa!"

CHAPTER 29

"Oh, balls," Dinah grimly intoned.

She was having the worst night of her life.

When she arrived at the café, a party was already in full swing. Glamorous people were drinking champagne and brutish pop music thudded out into the street.

A woman was being bundled out of the café, onto the pavement, and it seemed to be some sort of entertainment for some of the diners assisted in her ejection and the rest were amused by it. She helped the woman to her feet and retrieved the bundles of old newspapers that had fallen from the plastic supermarket bags she carried.

"Leave me alone!" the woman swung a bag at her and cried out in pain. "They have made a fool of me!"

She let her go but, when she went into her place of work and saw the amused looks of well-dressed people waiting for her to perform, she herself had a similar feeling.

"What has happened to all my friends? Why did you throw out that poor woman?" she said to the proprietor, an eerie son of the city, lately and unconvincingly fastened into a dinner jacket.

"We've gone up in the world," he sneered. "We don't need that kind of custom."

"That's no reason!"

"She had no money," he shrugged. "She had a smell off her like an elderly mackerel."

"She would have done no harm. It would have made her happy," Dinah argued.

"Ah, now, that's where you're wrong!" Her employer

chuckled and coughed around his cigar. "You can't please all the people. Our customers would have been most unhappy to have their supper overlaid by bodily pongs and our charity case would have had a more prolonged humiliation. Forget about it, Dinah, like a good girl, and get out your gospel. Your brethren await." He detained her a moment longer to show her a new pink neon sign, which was to replace the old display board outside the café. "What do you think?"

"Psalm's Place!" She read in gloomy disbelief.

"It flashes on and off!" he boasted.

She sighed, and got her bible out of her bag.

She read from Romans in chapter 13: "Love worketh no ill to his neighbour: therefore love is the fulfilling of the law."

After that she went off and phoned Figgis.

She waited while he dealt with some controversy adjacent to the telephone. "I am in the bosom of my family," he apologised; "and it has ears for tits."

"This doesn't require any complicated debate," Dinah said. "You asked me to go away with you. I am saying yes. All you have to do now is say if you meant it."

"Of course I meant it at the time," he said; "but I had drink taken. I can't just walk out on them at Christmas."

"Come away after Christmas."

"I am not my own man," he said. "You'd understand if you had children."

"Happy Christmas, Figgis," she said and she put down the speaking set to release him.

CHAPTER 30

"Who's been sleeping in my bed?" Dinah bellowed.

Alice, wrestling with wisps of some unpleasant fantasy, struggled into consciousness.

"A fecking nigger!" squealed Verity, who had just come from the bathroom to find Dinah glowering into the tangle of bedclothes. "She never said I'd have to sleep with a black."

They began, noisily, to squabble, and then hustled their dissent in on top of Alice.

"I'm not sleeping with her, I'm not sleeping with a black!" Verity wore nothing but a set of unwholesome-looking black lace undies.

"Why aren't you in your nightie?" Alice said sleepily.

"Why is she here at all?" Dinah said. "Is this your idea of a practical joke or is she supposed to be my Christmas present?"

"I haven't got a nightie. I've nothing. I may be rubbish but at least I'm white," continued Verity on a rising note.

"There must be something in your luggage." Alice, not fully awake, had become fixed upon the dilemma of the night attire.

"What luggage? I've got no luggage."

"Yes, you have, dear. I saw it. She's got a large canvas hold-all," she said to Dinah.

"Do you realise what kind of woman that is?" Dinah said.

"She is a homeless one. She is ... " Alice glanced apologetically at their unexpected guest; "a lady ... of the night."

"In my bed! I could get crabs."

The introduction of shellfish to the controversy confused

Alice further. She remembered sadly that they were supposed to have chips.

"You shouldn't have let her in," Dinah sulked. "She could have been a burglar."

"Yes, well, she's not," Alice said.

"How come you're so certain? What about this canvas bag she seems so fond of? Are you sure she is not just looking for a convenient place to drop off the loot?" Dinah's blood was up. "Hey, you!" She called to Verity. "Show us what you've got in that bag."

"What bag?"

"Your blue hold-all," Alice reminded her. "You were holding on to it for dear life."

Verity's lips drooped, too weary to make the scowl she attempted. "I had no bag. You must have imagined it." She turned her head aside and gave a long sniff.

"Now look what you've done," Alice reproached Dinah. "I thought you would be pleased to see me thinking of someone else for a change. I wanted to prove to you that I wasn't just a crusty old carbuncle."

Dinah softened. "I'm sorry. I'm the one who's crusty. It was a very wearing evening." She held out her hand to Verity. "Shake? After all, it is not the first time I have been abused for my colour nor, I am certain, the first time you have had an unwelcome visitor in your bed."

"My nerves are bad," Verity apologised, offering mauve fingers.

Dinah pumped the bony offering. "My name is Dinah. What are you called?"

"Verity."

"Ferrety?" She turned to Alice, her face squinched up with delight. "She says her name is Ferrety."

"It's *not* Ferrety!" The girl wailed. "Don't you make fun of me. It's Ferrety!" She stamped her foot and repeated her name. Alice couldn't prevent a small smile for the girl did

177

actually pronounce "v" with the sound of "f". Temper emphasised the sharpness of her little teeth, the arrow of her jaw.

Anyway it appeased Dinah and to Alice's relief she produced from her handbag an oppressed parcel of fried potatoes. Ferrety was too hungry to sustain a grudge. They both sat on the edge of Alice's bed and foraged among the sopping greaseproof parcels until only the crunchy rubble remained. "Those clocks in the hall," Ferrety negotiated salty crumbs; "why aren't they working?"

"They are working," Alice said. "I just forgot to wind them."

"Well, don't—not while I'm here."

The clocks seemed to have a strange effect on everyone.

"It's my nerves," Ferrety said. "I hate spooky noises."

Somewhere in the house, the cat gave a strange gurgling cry, oddly human. There was a brief, sawing sort of lament, like a sobbing sigh. Ferrety's long neck stretched until she resembled a flamingo. Her pale face seemed hollowed out with alarm so that one could see clearly the outline of a chip still stored in her cheek. The others watched with interest, too absorbed in her reaction to wonder what had caused the cat such horror and such grief. Her lips worked at silent speed to formulate some warning. In the end all that came out was an irritated murmur. "Bloody little shithead," Alice imagined she heard her say.

* * *

In the night the earth turned cold. Alice awoke to Christmas morning, to anticipation and a little hangover; and to a glittering web of weather that left delicate claw marks on her window and hid away the mischief of the weather.

178

Straightaway she ran to see her little plants. Miraculously they had not suffered. They seemed even brighter for the freshness of the festive air and wore their rim of frost like a collar of good lace.

She did not immediately go back indoors. For all its promise of fulfilment, the day rang out with challenge. More and more she liked it out here in the garden. The elements did not argue nor the flowers insist on making you see their point of view. As she came to be at peace, increasingly, she wanted peace.

When she did return to the house she found Ferrety up and doing something at the stove. She wore one of Dinah's nighties, an outsized cotton tunic. With the opening of the back door, it billowed like a windsock. It reminded Alice that the child had nothing to wear. She racked her brain until it offered a solution. "The big wardrobe!" she muttered, quite pleased with herself. "I'll have a rummage."

"You'll what?" Ferrety tested the milk she was warming in a saucepan, with her finger. Then, as if cooking was some strange and unreliable alchemy, she pushed up the sleeve of the nightie and lowered in her elbow.

"What are you doing?" Alice watched with interest.

For a moment she looked puzzled, even guilty. Her dripping elbow jerked up. "Milk!" she said quickly; "for coffee! I was going to bring you coffee in bed."

"But I'm up," Alice protested.

"Well, bloody go back!" Ferrety snapped. "Sorry!" she whispered as Alice shuffled off. "Oh, sorry." Alice turned and waited patiently, a little wearily. "It's just, I wanted to do something." The waif appealed to her. "You've been kind and I've nothing to give you."

"It's nothing," Alice said. The girl was more like her old self now. She even looked quite pleasant when she smiled. Alice tried to feel relieved, but all she could think was that Dinah had been right. This girl, this outsider, had upset the balance of things. There was no telling where they would end.

Ferrety poised her saucepan carefully on the edge of a ring. "You are kind, aren't you?" She advanced on Alice. "I never thought you meant it that night, when you said I could look you up if I was stuck. Honest to God, I thought I'd be out on my ear. But you're pure gold. You'd never turn away anything that hadn't a place to go."

The words were meant to be placatory but Alice felt threatened. She wished Dinah were up.

When Ferrety tried to touch her she backed away and quickly agreed not to turn away anything, ever.

"I'll never forget this," she promised.

"That's all right, dear." Alice patted the air. "I think I will take you up on your kind offer and go back and lie down for a bit. Coffee would be very nice."

She felt better once she was back in bed and tried to compose an order for the day. She really must find something for Ferrety, Verity to wear. She heard the girl coming up from the kitchen and began to hoist the pillows about to support herself. Ferrety did not come up the stairs. She paused in the hall and could be heard there fiddling about. Alice strained her ears and could have sworn she detected the rasp of a zipper. There was definitely something queer but she wondered if Dinah hadn't got the wrong end of the stick, if the girl hadn't brought an empty hold-all, preparing to fill it up with loot. When she thought about it, she didn't really care. Down in the hall Ferrety gave a sharp snorting cry and then cooed to comfort herself. She must have caught a finger or stubbed her toe. She heard her then, softly chuckling to herself. It was the chuckle of a flowing stream, self-concerned and insouciant. It was not the laugh of a fallen woman. After this brief interlude of oddness, Ferrety moved quite briskly, bringing coffee to Alice and to Dinah and then she took herself off to have a bath.

When she came back she was wrapped in a towel. Steam rose off the sharp edges of her shoulders. She looked different. Her scrubbed face showed pink and her damp hair was combed severely. It could be seen now that the sickly make-up she normally wore was used to a particular effect, to make her look more helpless and more accessible. Without it, she was a bony countrywoman, disappointed and edgy. The activity of her nerves curdled the atmosphere.

"We're going to mass," Alice babbled. "Won't you come— that is, if you're of the same persuasion?"

"Persuasion?" Ferrety snickered. "Bloody brute force, more like. Anyway there's not much call for my sort."

"Oh, you're wrong," Alice said. "The Lord loves a sinner. You could mend your ways." She was still full of curiosity about the girl's lifestyle. She wished they could resume the easy dialogue they had enjoyed in the alley at night, but something seemed to be crackling within the other, an anger or a plan, and she seethed with adrenalin.

"I could catch pneumonia too!" She scrubbed at her wet hair with a corner of the towel. "I've nothing to wear."

"Yes, I've thought of that." Alice was pleased to have something to contribute. "I thought we might find something in Mother's wardrobe."

"Your ma? Where is she?"

Alice blessed herself. "She is safe in the arms of Jesus."

Ferrety laughed. "A dead woman's clothes? That's horrible! Give us a look."

They went into the other room to excavate the giant cupboard. Alice had hoped for Dinah's help but her ally had made herself scarce and gone to the kitchen to set in motion the ponderous dinner.

She could never understand why Dinah tolerated the ancient costumes when most other influence of her parents had been excised from the house. Perhaps she was superstitious about them, believing that spirits nested and fluttered

181

like moths within their stiffening folds. Ferrety was different. She dived into the claustrophobic closet with its surging, silent community, its distant fragrances and intimate pungencies. Coat hangers yelped and chattered as she flung one section of clothing aside and the garments slid down like people in a shipwreck. She became a dealer, peering and pulling and rubbing and sniffing.

Alice waited for her to give her curious harsh laugh that was like a cat's laugh, if a cat could laugh. She was sure to find the styles quaint and despicable. She herself knew nothing about fashion, did not understand it to be an imitation and a parody of life so that what seems like innovation is just a roundabout journey to achieve once more the start of the cycle. Mother's long, dowdy wools and crêpes with pleated waists and fussy buttons, her lace blouses and baggy skirts, were once again in fashion.

Dinah came to see what was going on, smelling sweetly of thyme where she had been mixing stuffing for the turkey. She stepped in and deftly plucked Father's old dress suit from the wardrobe, and a high-necked blouse of Mother's.

Ferrety wasn't a beauty but she did look poignant behind severely cut black cloth and wilting ivory lace. Everyone was pleased except her. She wound her towel tighter and continued to paw through the wardrobe's elderly tenants until she located an old grey dress of Mother's and then at last she smiled, patting the grim fabric against her bones.

Christmas mass was lovely, the children in their woollens, clutching giant dolls and mechanical monsters which had been brought by Santa. Even the adults enjoyed a temporary suspension of disbelief. They wore eccentric additions to their clothing, Noddy hats and fur gloves like bears' paws and, when they shook hands for the gesture of friendship, there were conspiratorial grins as if to say that even friendship was acceptable because it was a children's day.

People were still smiling when they came out of the church.

182

Alice, steered by Dinah's loyal arm, beamed at everyone. She didn't usually do so. It is an offence to catch the eye of others when you are lonely. People smile too kindly and it causes tears which in turn promote discomfort and embarrassment. Now she was at liberty to smile and she did, with the certain hauteur of mothers who trail offspring grown larger than themselves. Up in the choir stall someone was still kicking a hymn out of the organ. Alice felt like a hero on parade, back from the wars, waving to the crowd while the band played and little children cheered.

When she saw her mother waiting for her in the church-yard, her smile fell off. She looked disgusted, tall and bony in her grey lisle stockings and lace-up shoes, her rat-grey dress, watching Alice making a fool of herself.

Her mouth wavered and she looked to Dinah in appeal.

"Well, if it isn't Ferrety!" Dinah called out. "And don't you look as pretty as a pick-axe!"

"Verity," Alice nagged nervously. "Her name is Verity." Of course she had known it was Ferrety after a second or two, but the realisation brought no relief. How had the girl assembled the exact outfit with which Mother, for many years, had renounced life? Where had she found the grey stockings and how did her feet adjust themselves so neatly to Mother's brittle shoes?

She came towards them with that stiff, remembered walk and looked over Alice in exasperation. "You look like a teacosy in that jumper," she said. She laughed then, her cat's laugh. "Well? How do you like it?"

"What is there to like?" Dinah demanded fiercely.

"My fancy dress. It's good, isn't it? I've always loved dressing up."

"What are you, Basil the rat?" Dinah said.

"I'm her mother, you black bitch."

"But ... how did you know?" Alice fought for calm.

"There's a photograph of your mother in the drawing

183

room, dressed like this. I knew it was your mother. She's the spit of you."

"No!" Alice clung to Dinah's arm. "Take me home."

Later she tried to persuade the child to change into something pretty for the party but she wouldn't. She said she was comfortable, that she felt like a lady for the day.

* * *

The party was timed for eight o'clock but guests began arriving at three when they were still rendering down the turkey. These were not frivolous revellers but people who were hungry and hoping for something to eat. There was an elderly man who lived in a city hostel since the death of his wife; a pregnant shoe-shop assistant who was afraid to go home and a young, tiny, timorous widow who appeared alone in the doorway and was followed in a rush by her five giant children.

In Alice's youth, the arrival of a guest during a meal had been a horrifying event. The visitor had to be hurried into the front room while the appalled diners blotted their mouths to conceal the evidence. Drinks or tea and biscuits would be brought into the cold parlour and Alice had to sit there feigning serenity, while her stomach snarled, and down in the kitchen the maid gnawed on whole chops or chicken legs.

In this new life no such ritual obtained. Another chair was brought forward, a fresh glass and plate and knife and fork. It was Christmas and there was plenty to eat. Dinah, with her experience in catering, had cooked enough potatoes to fill a bath.

They ate in the kitchen, by the fire, to the sound of the pudding thudding softly in its pot on the stove. Ferrety and the shoe salesgirl talked of the Christmases of their childhood

184

in the country. The old man and the young widow imagined sentimental pasts with their dead partners and Dinah smiled at Alice, while the cat reclined on her stomach and snapped her jaws at morsels of turkey. There was a moment, after they had eaten, when a thick, digestive silence fell and Alice became aware that Ferrety was watching her, that old look of derisive assessment that she knew so well from her mother. She jumped up and began to clear the table and when she came back with the pudding, sweating alcohol beneath its blazing twig, the instant was safely past and Ferrety cheered along with everyone else.

After lunch the widow went home with her children. The old man, worn out by the efforts of being sociable, craved his bunk at the shelter. Only the pregnant shoe girl remained and she fell palely asleep in a corner of the kitchen, her fingers slipping from the stem of her glass so that port swooped like blood onto her decent dress. Ferrety said she was sleepy too and took herself off to Dinah's bed where Alice thought she heard her crying gustily to herself. Dinah made Alice put her feet up at the fire and turned on the new telly so that she could compose herself for the party in the company of dancing girls and comics and swag-chinned tenors.

Into this satiate lull all good intentions and unsuspecting, fell the children—Ted and Donald and Marjorie and Andrea.

They knew the minute they knocked that something was wrong. The door had gone from green to yellow. Its mildewed brasses sparkled bold as cliché would have them. And the porch—dear old relic of a best-forgotten childhood, with ancient insects lurching within sagging webs—was all done out in sprigged wallpaper, and costly hothouse plants flowering with unchaste abundance upon the painted shelves.

And something else . . .

"This place is like an oven," Andrea grumbled while they waited for Alice to come out and explain.

Alice didn't hear them at first. She was absorbed in a magic

185

act on the television screen in which canaries were stuffed into various apertures of a man's clothes and reappeared out of a woman's cleavage, looking squashed and terrified. Then when she came to the door she was preoccupied and was surprised by the quartet of middle-aged gloom.

She stared at them, her vision still distorted by scraps of stricken lemon wings. She realised who it was and remembered that they always came at Christmas. "Children!" She proclaimed in guilt and disarray. She blocked their entrance until Marjorie prodded her way into the hall. "How lovely! Do come in."

They stood sweltering in the unrecognisable drawing room and gazed about the blushing walls, the cushioned chairs, the crackling flames of fire and jittery drops of blaze on top of candles. Ted wanted to sit down at the television and fall asleep in front of the fire. It was an impulse never before experienced in Alice's house. He kissed his aunt. "You've got the place nice," he said in his unimaginative way.

"Alice, have you had a seizure?" Marjorie spoke more directly.

"Just a bit of maintenance," Alice laughed it off although, as always, Marjorie made her feel afraid. "Let me get you a drink."

She opened a bottle of old Irish whiskey which had been left by the widow to pay for her meal. It had been the pride and joy of her late husband, although neither of them drank. She fetched glasses from the groaning festive board, generously fulfilling her function as hostess. "It didn't cost much." She indicated the décor with her eye as she passed around the drinks. "It cheered me up. It was all done with the help of friends."

"Very nice." Donald guzzled the contents of his glass. "Adds to the value of the house."

"I'm all right for money," Alice said.

"She must be burning it," Marjorie murmured. "This place

is heated like the Shelbourne Hotel."

"I haven't been burning it," Alice said. "As a matter of fact, I've got a little extra. It's for you." She joined her hands together and beamed at them. "I've got a surprise for you."

Reflexively the children handed over their parcels. Alice thanked them. Beneath the patterned paper she could feel the outlines of familiar gifts—a bottle of sweet sherry, a tin of talc, a box of Irish Rose assorted. She placed them on the table and went to the mantelpiece where the cards were propped up and candles nested in the holly and four pristine white envelopes poised themselves dangerously close to the flames.

"As you know, I had intended to remember you in my will ... "

Andrea shifted her suited buttocks and cast a signal of alarm to the others.

" ... but then I thought, what's the point of doing something nice for someone when they're dead and gone? I wanted to see you enjoying my will." She handed an envelope to each of her nephews and to their wives. The children watched their presents glumly, as if they might contain notice of dismissal, and then clumsily commenced to rip them open. Shock showed, followed by doubt and then desire when they saw the sums that were written on the cheques.

Donald looked as if he had seen God—and then ogled Alice as if witnessing some more homely ghost.

"It's all right, dear," Alice said. "I haven't left myself short. I took a little mortgage on the house."

Andrea rattled her cheque, getting used to it. "We'll have to pay it off in the end anyway," she told her husband.

"No, you won't," Alice said.

"Oh, girls, don't argue," Ted bravely begged. "This is marvellous, Auntie!"

Alice smiled at the poor, dispirited, youthless boy. "We

only seem to meet on solemn occasions. We never seem to celebrate!"

"Yes, thank you, Auntie," Marjorie said sternly. At once she turned to Ted. "She's mortgaged the house. God knows what sums are involved." Distressingly, she burst into tears.

Alice looked at the door for rescue but Dinah was downstairs doing the dishes. To her surprise, it was her own voice she heard, fairly firm: "There will be no debts. No more debts—not even those of duty." Why had she said such a thing? She must have had too much to drink. In any case it seemed to have an effect. Marjorie rattled her nose in a hankie and Ted, having taken his whiskey too peremptorily, gallantly assumed her emotional state. "After all, here you are all alone in the world, and perhaps not too long for it ... " He shook his head and a tear fell. He wiped it fastidiously away from the rim of his glass.

"I'm not alone in the world," Alice said.

"You have neither chick nor child," Andrea prompted.

"The point is, there has been a bit of a change. The point is ... you won't have to worry about the house any more because you won't actually be getting it."

"Found yourself a fellow, have you?" Donald joked, but both women hissed, "Shut up!"

"No. There is no fellow. I'm leaving it to Dinah."

For a minute they were too dumbfounded to think but then Marjorie blurted out, "Dinah? The cleaning woman?"

"Yes," Alice said, "that Dinah! She is not, in fact, the cleaning woman. I agreed to that version because I was ashamed. Loneliness turns you into a coward. You agree to any kind of a story that will stop people turning their backs. I'm all right now, I'm no longer afraid so I can say it straight out. Dinah is ... "

For a dizzying moment her tongue seemed to stick to the roof of her mouth and she was unable to make any more words. She was aware of the children's watchful gaze, waiting for her to make some slip that would verify the unsoundness of her mind. She felt as helpless as someone sinking into mud.

Dinah came in, neat and smiling, carrying a tray of tea. She put the tray down and turning to Alice, out of sight of the children, made a face of comic horror.

At once Alice was free to speak. "Dinah is my daughter!" she beamed at them all in relief.

* * *

There was singing, there was dancing, there was jubilation— not from the children, of course; they had retreated to a corner to discuss a manner in which they could best have their aunt committed. Alice was sorry about that. She would have liked to see them welcome Dinah into the family. She made every effort to reason with them but it was hard to match banter to speechless wrath. In any case the real visitors had begun to beat upon the door and Dinah had to go and let them in. Alice loyally dallied with her relatives until, out of nowhere, Arbroath Smokie appeared and swept her off in a waltz, his moustache shockingly crushed against her forehead.

After that the events of the day grew hazy. She was aware of intense happiness. She was awed by life's capacity for transformation, swift and unpredictable as the seasons. She was impressed by a similar facility in Ferrety, the fallen woman. From time to time in the midst of her drinking and singing, Alice would catch her mother looking at her from a corner of the room and for an instant she would feel fraudulent and abashed.

In other moments she became aware of a cluster of men buzzing in some part of the room but, when she came over for a closer look, she saw that it was Ferrety they enclosed;

Ferrety in her plain grey dress, but now laughing and teasing in a scornful manner so that men were drawn to her as a pin to a magnet.

CHAPTER 31

Dinah found the note when she was clearing up the following morning.

"Thank you for your kindness, past and future. What I have done may seem heartless but it is my only chance. I know you will act for the best. Yours, Verity. P.S. Look in the big clock—name of Wanda."

She knew Ferrety was gone. She heard her leaving in the small hours, but made no move. It was a free country, more or less, and she was not, anyway, a clement presence.

She and Alice studied the note over breakfast. "Do you have a clock called Wanda?" Dinah pondered.

"I used to give the clocks names when I was small. I don't remember a Wanda."

They had resorted to a refill of tea when they heard a noise from the hall. It was not an alarming sound but all the same they went out together.

"Look!" Alice said. "She forgot her bag."

Now that the confusion of Christmas was over, she saw it at once, wedged within the glass-fronted chamber of the grandfather, the blue holdall.

"There's something in it." Dinah peered. Even with its vivacious new décor, the hall did not admit much natural light. "It's quite a large something. The bag is open at the top. She couldn't get the zip to close."

As if to offer a clue a hand appeared in the aperture of the carrier and waved at them; a tiny hand, but emphatically human. At first they only stood and gaped for the shock of finding a live human where you least expect it is just as great as that of finding a corpse. The fingers waved in a clumsy grabbing fashion that compelled one to wave back but now Dinah was opening the door of the clock, pulling down the zip of the holdall and deftly removing a large infant child.

"It's a baby!" Alice exclaimed. "How extraordinary."

Even Dinah had to admit that it was. The child, quite unharmed apart from a neglected rash of long standing, had a composure which suggested she was used to sleeping in clocks and hold-alls and to being comforted by strangers. The tufts of her hair had been flattened by the pressure of her confinement and her dainty shells of nails had grown long and dirty. She stared at them with raw blue eyes and then slammed a dribbled paw into Dinah's face.

"You're Wanda, aren't you?" Dinah jiggled the child and it cackled. "You're Ferrety's big, bad secret. No wonder she was in such a state."

"It all adds up," Alice said in excitement. "This is why she didn't want the clocks wound. She was worried about the pendulum—like that story by Poe. She was always looking for milk. I wasn't going off my rocker. I did see her with a hold-all."

"Well, she's certainly left you holding the baby now," Dinah laughed.

"Yes," Alice said. "Oh dear."

"What's the matter? It's what you always wanted, isn't it? A real baby at last, a proper one—white and everything." Dinah's mouth nuzzled the baby's scrappy hair as she spoke. Across its skull she watched Alice's eye grow jealous.

"Oh yes," she said forlornly.

With her free hand Dinah reached into the blue bag and felt around. "At least her mother has not left her destitute." She pulled out a pack of nappies and a feeding bottle and some tiny clothes that looked like unstuffed toys. "Disposable underwear and a change of outfits! I'll take her to the bathroom."

She watched the jaunty swing of Dinah's behind up the stairs, the baby's feet dabbling the air as it wallowed on her hip. In the space of twenty-four hours she had acknowledged one daughter and acquired another. It was what was known as life's rich fabric, but it wasn't a ballgown she wanted at her age. Voluptuous sloshing sounds came from the bathroom and she heard Dinah singing. She was happy anyway. The baby seemed to suit her.

Alice could see the sense of that. It would be a reason for Dinah to stay. As she herself declined, the baby would get better and better. She saw them in the garden in summer, Dinah poking at her plants with a trowel and the baby in the green cradle, under the shade of apple trees.

After that she moved on instinct. She fetched the green cradle and lined the bottom with a folded rug. Two lacy tray-cloths were spread as sheets and a silk cushion set between them. On the top, Alice arranged her own new patchwork sweater, the sleeves folded underneath, so that it made a woolly quilt, soft and warm.

When Dinah came back with the infant, the little bed was ready by the fire and Alice was pouring heated milk into a bottle. Dinah was pleased. "You see how easy it is. As soon as you stop thinking about it, it comes." She sat the child on her knee and took the feeder from Alice. The baby drank with lusty sighs and then wandered idly into sleep, dropping sophisticated lashes onto sticky cheeks.

"What age do you suppose she is?" Dinah said.

"It's two months since I first met Ferrety and she must have had her by then so I suppose she is three or four months."

"Four months, then. She can have a birthday in the summer, in August."

"Your mind is a permanent whirl of parties," Alice shook her head. "How you can think of more festivities with yesterday's party barely cleared away! I myself did nothing and yet I am worn out."

"Take a nap," Dinah advised. "Follow Wanda's example. We don't have to do anything today except finish the turkey and watch TV."

"I am too unsettled. I'll just sit here and keep an eye on the child."

There is an exertive quality to a baby's sleep. Food fuels it and, beneath its cover, activity takes place, growth and furious mental adjustment to the continual shocks of its new waking life. To watch over a sleeping child is to be drawn into this process. So Alice, watching Wanda, began to drift. She thought she heard Dinah say something, or read something: "Behold, I show you a mystery. We shall not all sleep, but we shall all be changed." But perhaps it was just some voice that had crept into her dream.

She dreamed that she had wandered out into the garden and it was all in bloom. Heavy roses, pink and fragrant, dangled from their arched trellis. Scarlet tulips waded waist high in a fluttering froth of bluebells. Pears and apples thudded from their branches onto pastel tapestries of lily and freesia. She knew that several seasons were jumbled together but it seemed not so much a confusion as the resolution of some long-standing one. "The air has cleared," she thought in great relief.

In her dream she could not wait to wake up so that she could go into her garden and see if this was really so.

When she did wake, she was alone with the baby. Wanda had risen too and was staring at her. This recall to reality annoyed her for it seemed like a distraction from some more important matter, but, the dream having evaporated, she couldn't remember what that was.

"Gur," said Wanda, and she laughed.

A thought stole into Alice's head. She could pick her up. There was no one to see. She had not liked to do this when

Dinah was around, for babies tend to betray the inexperienced by bursting into howls. The notion became a longing, a grievance. Why shouldn't she have what other women have, the mindless love, the exquisite comfort? She imagined the feathery feel of a new human, still fluttery from prehensile wings left over from its recent angel state.

"Dinah!" She called out softly and was elated when she failed to reply. Cooing, she advanced. The child watched her with a wry look. She was not used to such talk. When she did not scream for help, Alice delved among the makeshift bedclothes and hoisted her out.

It was a surprise. It was not soft and sweet as she had thought. It was heavy; solid as a pudding. And damp. It did not cry but simply endured. Its stoic unappeal was a mirror to Alice's earliest past.

Earlier it had seemed quite a nice child but she could see now why Ferrety had hidden it in a clock. For such a large baby it had hardly any hair and it was not, to be blunt, fragrant.

She too had an impulse to hide it. She could not think what to do. It was growing heavier in her arms. It no longer felt like a human infant. It was like a baby pig.

The child's face began to change. Its features drew together and its snout wrinkled up and its eyes vanished into folds of flesh. It complexion turned the bright unwholesome ruby of a monkey's behind. It grunted. It actually grunted.

"Dinah!" Alice was becoming increasingly uncomfortable. "I think it's done something!"

"Dinah?" The silence that followed was an answer. Alice strained every fibre into that carrying blankness. "Dinah!" She cried out in panic. She began to understand. The pig bucked and squealed in her arms as she ran from room to room, calling.

195

CHAPTER 32

"What do you suppose she's thinking?" Marjorie said.

"Nothing. She's thinking nothing at all."

The children peered at Alice, their faces doomy as granite angels.

"She looks well," Donald said.

"Well?" Andrea was faintly appalled.

"Younger."

"She's only sixty-seven," Marjorie said, and she shuddered, feeling some chill claw that was already pointing at her own parts.

"Peaceful," Donald amended.

"Yes, well, she's had a very sheltered life." Andrea's aggrieved tone appeared, as ever, to offer argument, but it was only envy.

Sheltering Alice had become their duty. What else was there to do? One could not talk to her. Her wistful face pleaded ignorance. Her conversation made a dusty display of a life's collection of platitudes.

In recent times, Marjorie had wished she might confide in her, for there was no one else. What would she have said?

"Aunt, I have to have my two breasts cut off and I'm afraid. I feel like a bird whose wings are being pulled away."

She was not a poetic woman, but anyway that is how she felt.

Of course she did not say this to Alice. She had not told Andrea either for they were on cautious terms; and Andrea had not divulged to her that Ted's business was going to the wall and he was drinking heavily. They had no money, nothing to look forward to but the expectation of Alice's house.

Now they gazed down on their aunt in her peaceful sleep and felt an odd, lopsided grief with an aftertaste of resentment. She called them children, when no one else did. She had got off too lightly. Her harmless pink face with its vapour of grey curls had never been stamped with the anguish of battles, lost and lingering. Once again she had left them to do the worrying. It was a simple matter of domestic management; merely a matter of life and death.

The doctor called them in on Christmas morning to tell them that Alice had taken a turn in the night. The long sleep that followed her stroke had become the final stage of coma. He was sorry, but she was now technically dead.

"Technically?" Ted shouted in fear. "She's breathing, isn't she? There's nothing technical about breathing."

But there was. For the man in the white overall, like a butcher's overall, showed them the large machine that had taken over the business of Alice's breathing.

In his own way the doctor was kind. Since her seizure a month before, when she stole the limelight from some other old lady's funeral, she had lived in a world of her own, he said. It wasn't the world as we know it, of course, he put in hastily when Marjorie began to protest that their aunt had refused to recognise them when they made numerous, troublesome visits. All the same, she seemed happy. Now and then the nurses heard her laughing. On the night before Christmas she sang a verse of "Silent Night" and, before her final collapse, she seemed to imagine she had a baby.

"Why not leave her then," Ted said, "if she's happy?"

"It's different now." The doctor was firmer suddenly, and more professional. "There's nothing going on any more. Unplug the machine and it's all over."

"How do you know there's nothing going on?" Ted was stubborn.

197

"We have to accept medical findings. The machine is needed for sick children. It's just a formality, really, but we need the permission of next-of-kin."

It wasn't like taking a life, he assured them; no more than a neglect to mechanically sustain it—like deciding not to wind a clock. He glanced at his own healthy timepiece and left them alone to make their judgement.

"What a Christmas!" Donald glared out of the window at a cold, wind-flung rain that flattened itself against the glass.

"Yes," Marjorie said, her bruised mind retrieving for her an incident from the past in which she had taken a thrush from the jaws of a cat. She could not bear its rustling trawling of leaves with its damaged flight parts, one beady eye peering up at her out of a hopeless hiding place, and she had to kill it quickly with a spade.

"Yes," snapped Andrea, thinking of a costly Christmas dinner wasted, of all their bloody lives wasted, really.

Andrea felt a twinge of irritation when Ted failed to submit to the chorus. As usual his mind was elsewhere.

He was thinking of a time when Alice used to babysit him and Donald when his parents went out on their wedding anniversary. It was July and she always brought a bag of strawberries or cherries. She would sit on the front step in the evening sun while he and Donald biffed each other on the lawn. Sometimes she looked at a magazine. She couldn't have been more than twenty-five or so, only a girl—not pretty or anything, but nice. It was odd to think of Alice as the same species as the girls in the magazines he used to buy at airports, all peaks and curves and smiles. Andrea had never been like that. She had been so bright and ambitious that disappointment set in even before he failed. Alice had a stillness about her, sitting on the front step staring at the setting sun while he and Ted went mad on the grass, as if her head was stewing with dreams. What ever had she been thinking?

"What are you thinking, Ted?" Andrea demanded.

He turned from the window. "I was thinking, she's best off out of it. I think we should let her go."

"Well, that's blunt," his wife said, relieved. "Let's tell the doctor and then we can all go home."

He stuck out his chin and guiltily eyed the figure in the bed. "In a minute."

"Ted!" Andrea warned.

"We only see her once a year. It looks bad, rushing her. Give her fifteen minutes."

"Fifteen minutes for what?" Marjorie angrily wanted to know.

Ted crept over to the bed and peered upon his aunt, willing her to twitch or whimper or say a name, wanting, really, some sort of revelation. Her face was bland as a souvenir plate. The white hospital cover rose and fell its measured fraction. Only the machine that forced resuscitation upon her was busy and alert. "I don't know," he said miserably.

CHAPTER 33

She was thinking: "Dinah has gone!"

She knew that, of course, even as she ran through the house calling to her, the baby struggling in her arms. She lifted her muzzle and sniffed, like an old dog returning home and finding it deserted. The echo of her laughter was draining from the high parts of the house. In a while it would be hard to bring her face to mind.

Sooner or later everyone left; first her parents, then Mrs. Willoughby. Now Dinah was gone. Even the cat seemed to be missing. Her tour of inspection had revealed no black bulk glowering on hearth or hob. Perhaps Tiny had followed Dinah, like Dick Whittington's cat. She had been very attached.

"I have neither chick nor child," Alice cried aloud to the room, which indifferently belched back a stale breath of Christmas.

She remembered then. "I tell a lie!" There was the baby. After the initial shock of Dinah's disappearance she had put her down to sleep. Then she forgot about her. A baby was better than nothing—not much for conversation but other mothers might talk to her when she wheeled it out in the pram. She could pass the days in learning to knit and teaching it its prayers.

She returned to the kitchen and leaned over the green cradle. It was empty! She felt beneath the folded jumper in case Wanda had managed to make herself invisible in the way that cats do. The baby was gone. She must have flown away.

"Baby?" she said aloud. "What made me think of a baby? We never had a baby in this house. I must be dreaming." She plucked her sweater from the toy cradle and shook and folded it. "Now how did that get in there?"

There was a silence brewing. She could feel it watching over her, gathering itself ready to open its mouth and swallow her. *For what is life,* the thought drifted into her; *it is a vapour that appeareth for a little time and then vanisheth away.*

Where had she heard that? Dinah read it out to her. Dinah?

"I'm not ready," she thought in a panic. She would not let the silence take her. She would sing a hymn, if she could sing. Better yet, let Father sing it for her! She fetched the record in its age-scorched sleeve and lifted the lid of the gramophone. Then she stood there, a long time it seemed, looking in.

Father was lying in the box, his hands folded on his chest, one corner of his mouth lifted in a little smirk, as if he was playing a joke. She started back when he opened an eye and winked at her.

"Has she gone?" he said.

For a minute she could scarcely speak. Oh Lord, she was glad to see him. "Dinah?" she croaked. "Yes, she's gone all right."

He sat up smartly, rubbing his knees, peering around the room. "I was talking about your mother. She's gone, hasn't she?"

Alice thought about it. "Yes," she said. "Mother's gone."

"That's all right, then." He hauled himself up and began to swing his legs over the edge of the box.

"Have you been here all along?" She offered him an arm for support.

"Yes." He sprang nimbly on to the floor. He was just as she remembered him, small and wiry and badly dressed. "I was waiting for you."

How could she express her gratitude? Hospitality, perhaps, was the keynote. "Would you like something to eat? There's turkey left."

For a moment he looked startled and she thought he shuddered. "No, thank you—nothing at all."

"Haven't you got your teeth in? Something soft, perhaps?"

"No, Ally, no." He had forgotten all about that part of life, when he used to sit down and eat with relish a winged creature or an animal.

"What would you like, Papa?" She had him to herself after all those years. He was calling her Ally, as he used to when she was a little girl. She wanted to appeal to him.

He put his arm through hers. "I'd like to see the garden."

She opened the door and the wind came in. She hurried to button up her cardie but then she noticed that the breeze did not touch her skin. It affected only her sense of smell.

It was bringing her perfume; dizzy humming scents of summer roses, the pepper of nasturtium and the violet's whispering aura of romance. She sensed the high, pure tone of lavender and the swooning breath of honeysuckle. Father sniffed happily. "You've done all right, Ally." He patted her arm and led her outside.

"I didn't do the garden, Papa." She hung back, ashamed of how little she had achieved.

"I know that." He turned to look at her and she was surprised to see that he approved of her. "All the same, you've done all right.

Fleshy roses curled into the stone wall and hollyhocks nestled at its base. Dusky red poppies bent into their path and the flimsy pink flowers of cherry swarmed on a blue sky. A magnolia yielded its curdy petals and they spun slowly down, satin and cream, pallor and blush, twirling and touching, piling up on the path like dancer's slippers in a dressing

202

room. "Oh!" Alice cried, imagination failing her as usual, "it's
... heavenly."

The cat's eyes in the crazy paving winked up at her and
father smiled.

CHAPTER 34

"Hell!" Dinah swore.

She could not get her suitcase to close. She had broken her own rule by buying an extra overcoat and now she found she had more possessions than would easily fit in a single case. She removed the squashed items of luggage and placed them on the bed, reviewing their usefulness. Carefully, she folded her old anorak around her bible and laid it in the case beside the economical roll of her spare blouse and skirt. With less attention she tucked in an envelope containing all her money, several thousand pounds, which she had removed from the bank in cash. She revised the remaining contents and then thoughtfully took the spanner and placed it on the bedside table for someone else who might find it profitable.

When she had successfully fastened her case and checked the room she went to have a last look out of the window. Small bits of rubbish fled about, freed from the seething human tide, the squelch of traffic and its black halitus. She would have liked to see some signs of life—a person or a dog or even a rat. Everyone was somewhere else. The streets had been erased of sound.

Her new friends were reunited with their families, at least for the duration of the holiday. Even her fellow lodgers in the run-down hotel had attracted some welcome. The toothless, the alcoholic, the absent-minded had all found a place and gone off, paper bags stuffed with cheer, rattling and clanking. They were smarter than she would have thought. Foxes have holes.

As a last resort she had telephoned Alice, who had once

been kind to her and offered her a room under the eaves, papered with newspaper. Some relative answered, a woman with a voice like vinegar, and said that Miss Boyle had died peacefully in hospital earlier that day.

She had one more call to make and then she was on her way. Quickly she seized her bag and went down to the hall to use the phone.

"Figgis?" She poised her tenpences on the slide when she heard his voice.

"Is that you?" He spoke gently. "Sweet black narcissus?" A child yelled in his background and she heard his muffled remonstration and when he came back the irritation stayed in his voice. "Sweet suffering Jaysus. Don't you know better than to ring a man at home at Christmas? Here I am, up to me oxters in reconciliation."

"I know all that," she said. "You told me all of that. I just wanted to say something."

"I'm a worm. I'm a cur."

"That is not what I wanted to say. I wanted to tell you, I'm going home."

She could feel his apprehension. "And where, may I ask, is that?"

"Africa."

The faint bark and squawk of his family was contained, like a little barnyard, within the radius of her listening. He had covered the phone again and she heard him whisper something, softly this time, and she imagined that his wife had come out to examine his stunned back, to try to make something of it, and that he had turned his head and asked her to go off into the kitchen and make him a cup of tea.

She endeavoured to make a picture of his kitchen but solitude confined her vision to the place where she was interned and all she saw was the hotel's entrance, its walls painted to halfway in an injurious shade of red and then in spattered cream up to the ceiling where the gentrified mouldings of its Georgian origin were marooned with spider and beetle and anything else that could not be got at.

She couldn't think what else she might say, or what he might say, so she hung up and went out.

It was an agreeable day for walking, cold and quiet, with all the shops closed and little thorns of tinsel scrabbling through the metal shutters. Ropes of Christmas lights winked bravely over wastes of grey.

She found a place that was open for breakfast and sat at a counter next to an old man who slurped coffee from a cardboard cup.

"You could open another café," said a voice in her head. "Run it any way you want. You have money in your hand and you are your own woman."

"No." She was firm. "I am going home."

She moved on to Marlborough Street Church and lit a little flat candle like a peppermint cream in a blue votive lamp at the shrine of St. Joseph. All the other saints had progressed to electricity.

"Home to what?" God provocatively parried, when she had given Him her news.

"To my people."

"Are you sure they want you?"

"Of course they do. They need someone to speak for them. I have learnt how to talk to people and I'm black, like them."

"Tiny the cat is black," He pointed out, good-naturedly enough; "yet it is doubtful the Third World would welcome her with open arms."

Well, He was bound to be in a funny mood so soon after Christmas. She would not hold it against Him. She struggled from her knees and went out into the narrow lane where beggars collected pennies in boxes and the smell of roasting coffee from Bewley's Café was profligate as a burning garden.

Other people were in the street now, men dragging children and young boys and girls in their loose bright clothes. She went to St. Stephen's Green and sat on her favourite bench and fed her breakfast roll to the ducks.

"Home to the valley of my mother," she determined: For her mother had given her the only thing she had, her past. She had lost everything else, her firstborn child, Damien, her two and a half husbands, as well as the country of her birth.

She had Dinah, of course (or Cora, as she had been christened, but she preferred Dinah now), but she was only a daughter and a constant reminder of misfortune. Alone, abandoned with a small baby in a strange land, her mother had no opportunity to go back home. Dinah owed it to her to make that journey.

It occurred to her now that she did not know exactly where home was. Her mother had bequeathed her all her history but very little in the way of geography. She did not know the name of the order of nuns who had taught French to the child who would later give her life, and brought her as a treat to meet the lepers.

She had scarcely any information about her father. When she questioned her mother about him it always provoked a flood of tears and a hunt for the gin bottle. "You are too like him!" That was all she would say. "You have brains but you have no heart." Oh, well! Who would blame her? Poor little Mother with her heart broken and her homeland gone. The pang of pity Dinah felt was replaced quite unexpectedly by a surge of something like resentment. It was the sudden realisation that she, Dinah, was in exactly the same boat as her mother, except that she did not immerse herself all day in gin and self-pity. Her mother had been no older than she was now when Dinah, nine years of age, had to stay home from school to keep her clean and comforted. What had her mother really done with her life? All day long she sat around stroking her thin brown arms, telling her stories of nuns and brothels and dead babies, drinking and sighing, drinking and sobbing.

"My mother was a lush!" Dinah said, out loud and angrily.

When she was sixteen Dinah met a boy and fell in love. She got pregnant but her mother said she could stand no more misfortune and made her get rid of it.

There is no argument to tears. Dinah returned obediently home and looked after her mother until she died. Of what? She was only sixty.

"Idleness!" She bitterly exclaimed.

Some children came and skulked around her bench, mad with boredom. She gave them bread to throw to the ducks and they ran to the water's edge, mad with delight.

An elderly woman sidled onto the seat beside her. "I got better than that." She eyed the remains of Dinah's bread roll. She opened her bag and revealed a secondary compartment of paper, squashed and reeking. "I got scallion sangwiches." She frowned when Dinah's desolate look swept over her, but only for a moment. "I know a place where we could get booze," she ingratiated.

Somewhere in the park a rock band began to play and Dinah felt an odd sensation, not just the beat of the music in her toes, but a feathery whirr underneath her breastbone. She was beginning to feel better.

Perhaps it was the shedding of illusion, or else the simple warmth of human contact so lightly offered to strangers in this small city which saw itself as the slovenly kitchen of the Virgin Mary.

She felt ready now, to go. She held out a hand to her new friend. "Goodbye."

The woman did not take the hand but looked at it, her eye both vague and ponderous, as one lighting on a glove in the gutter and remembering the historic role of such a one in the wardrobe of one's past.

"Elsie," she said.

She brought her gaze to Dinah's face. "Elsie!"

Dinah took her hand away. "I'm not Elsie."

"It's my daughter!" She cried out to the startled children at the pond, to the aimless lovers and brooding, thirsting fathers.

"No!" Dinah got up quickly. "I'm not Elsie." She was gentle but firm. "You'd better just forget about Elsie."

She walked away with her head down and her hands in her pockets, knowing people were staring at her. Lord, what a place, what a day! She wished she had at least extracted the name of the place where one could get booze before being forced to move on. Come to think of it, if the woman had not made such a rumpus, she would have been interested to hear about Elsie.

She had gone about twenty yards when she realised that something was awry. It was to do with her hands. How could both be in her pockets when one should be carrying a suitcase? The answer did not exhaust the intellect but only the patience. She had left the bag behind her at the bench. Now she would have to go back and defend herself all over again against the identity of absent Elsie.

But when she turned around the bench was deserted. The woman was gone. So was her suitcase with all her possessions and her new-found wealth. Through the trees she spotted a meagre figure hauling a large suitcase, an aspect of triumph to her scuttling heels.

"Hey, you!" Upon Dinah's cry the swindler slowly turned. The two women's eyes wistfully engaged and the thief endured a moment's awful wavering before renewing her progress.

Angrily, Dinah watched her go. Could no one be trusted? Not Figgis? Not even a strange and lonely old lady?

Not even Elsie?

The woman struggled with the suitcase, her jaunty gallop dwindled to a dislocated trudge.

For a time Dinah stayed where she was, keeping vigil and then in due course she moved off. Swiftly and silently through the frozen park, she began to stalk after her mother.